Book III

A Novel

Billie Dureyea Shell

Dedication

This Book is dedicated to my
wonderful loving mom
Thank you for never giving up on me
Thank you 4 always being there
There is not enough words in
the English language 4 me to
express how much I love you but
know this I will always have your
back just like you always had mine
I Love You Mommy this one is 4 U

Team Shell

ACKNOWLEDGEMENT

This year has really a Mutual Fuckka Co-Vid ain't going nowhere.... But Fucc Co-Vid 19 we ain't going to let it stop NOTHING. So with that let me first and formost give thanks to my heavenly father for making it possible for my family to be okay during this pandemic and for all of us still being here healthy, Lord without you none of this would be possible to my mom I love you with all my heart it's because of you that I'm here and it's because of you that I'll always give 100% , keep my head up and know that I'm the head and not the tail, I love you Momma to my little sister Glenda what's up Blackie I miss you and I love you. To my wife Shatoya thank you for loving me and teaching me how to be more patient I love you with all my heart we got 10 kids you crazy if you think we having another one lol I'm good I got a hold on to the little bit of

Sanity I have left smile plus you drive me crazy enough... To All My Children I love you all and know that y'all the reason that I smile to my uncle Woody I miss you and I love you so much thank you for teaching me how to be a man to my brother Lawrence Mc Cloud I love you thanks always having my back to my brother Fred, I told you I was going to do it, to my sister Needra I miss u and love u little sister Bre I always got u...... to my brother and cousin Zane your missed every hour of every second of every day rest in peace we'll be together soon my nigga I got a few more things I got to do down here. To all my readers in the fans I love you all if it wasn't for y'all my dream couldn't have came true thank you for buying my books and reading them thank you all for letting me know how much y'all appreciate my writing skills and what I do its because of y'all that these books can't stay in stores and I'm going to keep on doing this writing shit as long as y'all wanna read it. With that much I'll let u get to this book I hope you all enjoy it let me know what you think I love all y'all

Author

Billie Dureyea Shell

Prologue

LA'DRAYSHA

I smiled as Nurse Myers entered my room, as she'd been so nice to me these past few months since I'd taken up residence in the hospital. She had replaced the first nurse I was assigned, an incompetent fool who was slow about everything and always interrupted when my mom came to visit. "Do you always have to wear that mask when you come in here, sweetie? Is my cancer contagious?" I asked coyly. "No ma'am. I tell you this every time," the nurse quipped. "I'm a huge germaphobe." "And I ask you this every time... why did you choose to be a Nurse? And how come, when I ask for you after certain hours, people tell me I'm crazy?" I responded. She looked at me but didn't respond. "Have you spoken to your mother lately?" she asked, changing the subject. My cancer had spread to my brain which caused a tumor they told me was inoperable, not to mention I was slowly recovering from a stint of amnesia. They said that I was only seeing my mother due to the tumor. Sometimes the medication would keep her away for a few days, but she always came back when she wanted to see me. "No," I sighed. "I think I made her mad. She wanted me to get rid of Betty Mae." Nurse Myers looked at me as if I'd just confessed to murder. "And what did you tell her?" she asked, raising an eyebrow. "I told her I was done with that family," I stated stubbornly, leaning back on the fresh pillows Nurse Myers had placed behind my back, the coolness seeping through the thin material of my hospital gown. With the arrival of new pillows, my bed was more soft and comfortable. I considered drifting off to sleep ... and that's when mama appeared. "Girl, you shut up. Don't trust this nurse. It's going to end real bad for you," mama warned. I rolled my eyes. I hadn't seen Nurse Myer's face but I trusted her. She made me feel comfortable and seemed to really care as she talked to me about my life and my love for Jamie, who made sure to visit daily. He never stayed real long but I was always glad when he showed up. My brothers had also come by and sent flowers, along with Tina, so I felt like I would truly be missed once I passed away. I hated that I was about to earn my wings, leaving these people who loved me so much. "My mama just told me not to trust you," I told Nurse Myers who also found the warning to be funny. She laughed and the sound was very familiar. It was in that moment, I realized that I'd never really heard her laugh. "Oh, no. You can trust me," she said, assuring me as she walked over to the IV. "The doctor has ordered you a dose of Levaquin." She inserted the needle into the injection port, allowing the medication to circulate through the IV tubing and into my blood stream. My body immediately began to grow numb and within seconds, I could no longer move. "What are you giving me?" I stammered in a voice that was hardly above a whisper. I watched, my body no longer responding, as Nurse Myers pulled another needle from her pocket and removed the cap. I could see it was already filled with some form of liquid. "You won't feel a thing," she promised, lifting the surgical mask she always wore. I looked into her familiar eyes, seeing her for the first time. I couldn't believe she was doing this to me. "Die slowly," she said as she walked away.

NINE MONTHS EARLIER....

Chapter 1

DANDRIDGE

walked into Sharon's room holding our son. I never realized they would have the DNA test results back so quickly. "You see mommy?" I asked the nameless boy as Sharon struggled to open her eyes. "Why do you have my son?" she asked. "Well ...about that," I started to explain but stopped, unable to bring myself to tell her. "We need to give him a name. I like Elijah." "We?" she questioned, looking more confused than ever. Instead of trying to explain, I pulled the piece of paper out of my pocket that held the results of the DNA test. I couldn't help but wish my genes weren't so strong because Maxwell never would have known he wasn't the father, had it not been for the resemblance. In fact, this little boy looked as if I could have given birth to him myself. Sharon's eyes grew big as she read the piece of paper, her eyes filling up with tears as she began to cry. "But... but your mother promised me it would be Max's baby. What happened?" she sobbed, crying as if someone had died. "I've run this man's name in the ground and it's not his? I ruined his relationship with my sister. All of this... just to end up with your baby?" "I'm not such a bad alternative," I responded indignantly in an effort to defend myself. "You're the worst alternative!" she said and then immediately, her voice softened and she apologized. "I'm sorry, Dan. It's just that I don't want my baby being a part of your family. Your mother is the devil." At least she was honest about her feelings, I thought. "Okay, I get that ...but the reality is that he is and we need to name him." I kept my cool because I didn't really want this either, but there was nothing that could be done to change things now. Sharon must have been thinking the same thing as she wiped her eyes. "You can tell them a name and I'll go with it," she sighed with indifference, turning her back to me. "Now, can you leave me alone please?" I took my son back to the nursery and gave him his name. "Dandridge Elijah Harris," I told the nurse. She gave me a look like that was the worst name she'd ever heard. "Why are you looking at me like that?" "The name doesn't flow is all," she muttered, rolling her eyes as she recorded the name. I didn't care how it flowed. That was his name, but we'd call him Elijah instead of Dan.

*****

"Ey!" I heard Maxwell's voice as soon as I walked out of the hospital. "What's up, man?" I turned toward his voice just as his fist made contact with my mouth. "What the fuck," I yelled as I touched my lip and saw blood on my fingertips. Max looked like a mad man as he started to deliver another blow. I dodged the punch and connected my own to his jaw. He took two shots to my ribs and I fell to my knees. The next thing I knew, he was on top of me, beating me like I'd stole something. "You son of bitch," I heard him say before Harvey pulled him off of me. "Let it go man," Harvey said to him as I struggled to stand on my feet again. "You're dead to me," Maxwell hissed as he glared at me. Several moments passed before he seemed to accept Harvey's advice, turning his back to me as he walked toward the parking lot. "Thanks," I said, turning to Harvey as I brushed concrete dust off my favorite pair of jeans. "I didn't do that for you, man. He's about to marry my daughter and I don't need him going to jail for murdering you," Harvey said, turning to catch up with Maxwell. "Damn, I can't even go get a change of clothes," I said aloud to no one in particular. I was going to stay overnight at the hospital to help Sharon with Elijah. I wasn't the best help to Cecelia with Danielle so I promised myself that I would be more supportive this time. Sharon wouldn't have to face being a new mother all alone. After all, she didn't ask to be put in this situation.

Chapter 2

MAXWELL

"I can't believe you just did that!" Shanice was talking to me but I didn't care about what she was saying. Fuming, I borderline wanted to kill Dan. How could he not tell me that his little hypothetical question from the bowling alley wasn't really hypothetical at all? I knew that nigga was holding on to secrets but damn! How could he let Sharon pin that shit on me when he knew better? "I'm not in the mood to argue about this," I told her. "I don't care what mood you're in, Max. You didn't have to put your hands on him." I looked at Shanice like she'd lost her mind. "That man allowed this girl to go around talking about how I wasn't trying to be a father to my child. He slept with my woman and tried to make jokes about it, and he had an entire family while stringing you along and I didn't need to put my hands on him?" I reasoned, lifting one brow. I couldn't believe she didn't think he deserved that ...and more. "I wasn't your woman when we slept together," she said, almost under her breath. "If I wasn't a gentleman, your ass would be walking," I said out of anger. I couldn't believe her. "Really?" She looked at me like she was shocked by my words, but I didn't respond. I loved Shanice but I had nothing more to say to her at the moment. As we pulled up to the house, Shanice slammed my car door and walked in the house like she was trying to make a statement. I didn't care anything about her attitude, so I sat there for a little while, thinking and reflecting on everything that had been happening lately. I turned on my radio and it seemed as if the Kenny G radio knew exactly what I needed to hear as I listened to Dana Glover singing to the sound of the sax, played by Dave Koz. "But as long as you are breathing You can start all over again If your heart's beating You can start all over again Goodbye to sorrow, you can start all over again Hello tomorrow, you can start all over" I picked up my cell phone and placed a call. "I'm not going to Drum," I told Jackson as soon as he answered the phone. "Are you trying to get kicked out this Army?" I could hear the frustration in his voice. "Yes," I answered honestly. "Okay, man. It's on you. I'm going to make some phone calls and see what they want to do. I'll let you know," he said as he hung up. I needed a new start with Shanice and a regular life. I wanted to pursue my music and I knew it wasn't going to be easy, but I at least had enough money saved up to get me and Shanice through for about two years. I walked into the house and found Shanice in the bedroom, watching the Steve Harvey show that she'd recorded. "Can we talk?" I asked. She acted as if I hadn't said a word but I continued, knowing she could hear me. "I love you, Shannie, and I'm not trying to mess this up. I'm sorry for my attitude toward you in the car," I apologized, even though I didn't feel that I needed to. "It's fine," she responded, but I could tell by the tone of her voice that she didn't really mean that. "I'm serious, Shanice. I don't want us mad at each other. There is enough going on without us walking around mad." I sat beside her and reached for her hand. "I'm going to be honest. I really want to make love to you, but I know that's not an option right now so can you please accept my apology and cuddle up beside me?" I looked at her with pleading eyes. "Okay," she sighed as her resistance diminished, moving closer to me. I kissed her cheek and started watching the show with her.

Chapter 3

LA'DRAYSHA

"They're not going to stand by you," my mother said. Her words stung my heart, nearly taking my breath away. "They will!" I countered. "They're my children and even though we've had our differences, they love me mama. They'll be by my side through this." "They hate you, girl! Do you know what you've done to them? And that ungrateful Danae? Now she ...she should love you." "She does love me. You think I'm going to tell them I have cancer and they're just going to let me die alone? Won't happen," I reasoned angrily, knowing my mother would never understand. I knew I had done some horrible things in my life, but I also knew that I'd raised my kids to have good hearts even if they didn't really know how to use those hearts. I picked up my cell phone and quickly sent a text message to all three of them. "Meet me at the house tonight at 8. It's very important. I love you." I said the three words they never believed coming from me, but it was true. Danae had detached herself from me years ago, after her boyfriend was killed in a car accident. She had always blamed me, although it wasn't my fault at all. I was fairly certain that the other two, Dan and Carla, just put up with me because I was their mother and they were going to respect the position, if nothing else. None of them text back, but I was sure they would show up tonight. I sat across the table from Jamie, who hadn't spoken in nearly ten minutes. "Well, are you going to say anything?" I asked. "Marry me," he said. I looked around the dimly lit restaurant we'd chosen to see if anyone else had overheard his ridiculous request. "I just told you that I'm dying," I responded. "You also told me that you love me," he answered softly, "so I don't see the issue." He reached across the table to take my hands into his. "Look, Draysha. I know all about you and all the bad shit you've done, and I still love you. Let me love you to death. Let me take care of you while you still have time," he pleaded. "Okay," I smiled, "when?" "Now," he said as he pushed his seat back from the table to stand. "Right now?" I gasped, the expression on my face filled with surprise. A part of me had believed his absurd request was merely intended to make a dying girl happy. I hadn't thought he'd actually go through with it. "Yes, right now! We're both neatly dressed and all we have to do is call a couple of people to be our witnesses." He was smiling from ear to ear and I was ecstatic. I had no idea that my telling him that I had cancer would lead to his request to marry me, and take care of me in my darkest hour. "Okay," I laughed. "Let's go. I'll call Tina and Rowland and have the two of them meet us." I felt like a kid in a candy store. I was going to get my happiness ...even if it were just for a moment. **** Jamie and I walked hand and hand, wearing the broadest of smiles as we stepped through my front door. I was elated to be his wife. "What did you call us here for now?" Danae asked with obvious attitude, one hand on her hip for effect. Dan and Carla sat silently on the couch staring at me. "Drop the attitude," Jamie snapped, coming to my defense. "Who are you supposed to be?" She challenged Jamie, lifting one brow. "That's my real dad," Dan responded before I could answer. "Well, actually he's my husband!" I yelled out with excitement. "I can't believe this shit," Dan mumbled as he stood, looking at both of us like we'd lost our minds. "But that's not why I called you here," I sighed as I took a seat in the chair closest to my coffee table. "I'm here because I need to start making arrangements. I have breast cancer. I don't know how bad it is yet, but I believe that my condition is probably very serious." I thought about how I'd been seeing and speaking to my mother. "I'm including you all in my will. I'll speak to my attorney tomorrow about the previous revision and change it back," I informed them. "Nah, you good," Dan said in a matter-of-fact tone. "Dan, I'm sorry. I love you, son," I was genuinely apologetic for the hurt I had caused. He looked around the room, smirking as he noticed the stunned looks on Danae and Carla's faces. "I'm going to be honest. You can just die ...I could care less. At least then, I could live my life without you fucking it up at every turn. Good luck to you and this bastard," he spat, swinging his arm angrily through the air. "Don't call me again," he added, standing to leave as tears welled up in my eyes. I knew I had done some terrible things, but I thought my kids loved me even in spite of those things. Boy was I delusional. "I'm sorry you're dying but it looks like you will have all the support you need in your new husband, so if that's all you had to tell us, I'm going to go. I think my brother needs a friend right about now." Carla stood to follow Dan and I became angry. "Her brother needs a friend," I repeated in barely a whisper. Danae didn't say a word. Instead, she stood and placed one hand on my shoulder as if to say she cared a little before walking toward the door. "They hate me," I cried, looking at Jamie with tears in my eyes. "They don't hate you, Draysha. They may hate some of the decisions you've made but they don't hate you, they'll come around" he explained in a soothing voice, embracing me as my sobs grew louder and louder. I couldn't remember the last time I'd cried like this. I did the best I could by my children and here they were, walking out on me when I needed them the most.

Chapter 4

DANDRIDGE

"**O**ften one finds one's destiny just where one tries to avoid it." –Chinese Proverb I walked into Sharon's hospital room and sat in the chair facing diagonal to her bed. The nurse informed me that she had requested that our son sleep in the nursery that night. She'd also told the nurse that she didn't want any visitors, but I convinced the stern woman to let me remain with her anyway. I watched Sharon as she slept and the way the moon crept into the window, I noticed how beautiful she really was. I shook my head thinking about all that my mother had put this family through, a family of truly amazing people, people who didn't deserve the evil my mom brought their way. "I'm sorry," I said in a tone that was barely audible but Sharon still heard me. "Sorry for what?" she asked as she opened her eyes to look at me. "I'm sorry for not telling the truth when I had the chance. When you told me about the artificial insemination, I should have told you then that you were carrying my child. I knew," I admitted, realizing I had to finally start telling the truth. "I'm also sorry for the hell my mom put you and your family through, but I want you to know that I'm going to be there for my child, and for you ...if you will allow me to be in your lives." A tear rolled down her right cheek. "It's okay. What's done is done, and I won't keep him away from you," she spoke in a voice that was soft and low. "You're his father." I let out a long hard sigh. "Thank you, Sharon." She turned away for a moment and then asked a question I'm sure everyone would have liked to know the answer to. "Why are you such a liar?" My eyes widened in shock. No one had ever seriously asked me that. "I don't know. My mom kind of raised me like that. She lied to us all the time because she felt the truth would reveal too much or mess things up." "Wow," she said. "I think you should be honest more often. You might not be viewed as such a fucked up individual." Sharon was blunt and apparently very honest when given the opportunity. I liked that. "Well, maybe I'll try it. I'll try to be honest with you at all times, no matter what." I flashed her one of my most charming smiles. "Yeah, good luck with that," she said as she smiled back. My heart dropped at the realization she was absolutely gorgeous. "You might be a pretty cool baby mama," I laughed. "Yeah, I might." She kept that smile on her face and for a while, we just sat in silence. This wasn't an ideal situation, but it was one we'd take a day at a time.

*****

I stood, knocking on the door of the condo I'd given to Cecelia and it felt weird because it was once a place I could just stroll in or out of at will. She answered the door with Danny right on her heels. "Daddy!" she yelled, hopping up and down as if she could jump high enough to land in my arms. I immediately picked her up. "Hey, little girl. I missed you!" I spoke truthfully. It had been a few days since I'd seen my little girl, and after Sharon giving birth a few days ago, I'd been at her house with her and my son. "Cecelia, we need to talk," I said as I put Danny down. "What now, Dandridge?" She seemed annoyed already. I walked over to the couch and gestured for her to sit down, and that's when I noticed her suitcases by the entertainment center. "You moving?" She laughed. "Did you really think I was going to stay in a place that you shared with Shanice? I just needed to stay until I found something else ...and I did. I will return your keys on Friday." "Okay," I agreed, not wanting to argue. I only wanted to tell her what needed to be said, and then be on my way. Hopefully with Danielle in tow. "Look, Cecilia. I have a son-" She rolled her eyes and interrupted me. "How many more secrets do you have, Dan? You were cheating on me with more than just Shanice?" She just knew she was right when she really wasn't. "No. It's a very long story, but he was born a few days ago. Shanice's younger sister, Sharon, is his mom and no, we never slept together. My mom did some crazy shit and now I'm the father or her child. I came by to tell you about him, and also to ask if I could take Danny over to meet her little brother," I said, choosing my words carefully while pleading with my eyes. "First tell me if it's safe because you look like someone has been trying to kill you," she accused, making reference to the bruises on my face from Maxwell's attack outside the hospital. "It's safe," I answered, downplaying the whole ordeal. "Maxwell hit me." "Okay, I guess she can go," Cecilia answered, seemingly satisfied with my response. "I'll pack her a bag." As she stood to go pack Danielle's overnight bag, I watched her walk into the bedroom and I couldn't help but smile a little. I had to admit that I did have two fine ass baby mamas. As I took Danny by the hand and began walking toward the door, Cecelia called my name. "Dandridge?" "Yes?" I prayed she hadn't already changed her mind about me taking my daughter. "Thanks for being honest." She flashed me a smile. "It's something new I'm trying." I closed the door behind me and smiled. Telling the truth felt so much better than all the lying.

Chapter 5

SHANICE

I stepped into the house a little after eight and noticed that the entire place was filled with candlelight. I heard the sound of Maxwell's keyboard and slipped off my heels, heading in the direction of that beautiful music. I paused in the doorway as I listened to the song he was playing, the lyrics pouring out of him as if he'd felt the words inside of his soul. "Lord, I Lift her up to you, There are some things I can't do, She has a void, That I can't fill, And she has some tears, I can't wipe away, Hear me when I pray, As I lift her up to you." He sang with such passion, that tears welled up in my eyes. I knew Maxwell was carrying this burden with me and that he cared, but I hadn't realized he cared so much that he'd sing about it. "That's beautiful,"

I said with awe in my voice, and he jumped as if I'd startled him. "Thanks. It's from the Scared Love Songs album by T.D. Jakes, but I feel those words daily," he admitted, speaking softly. I lowered my head but didn't say a word. "That wasn't the song you were supposed to hear me singing though," he added with a smile. "Well, what song was I supposed to hear?" He gestured for me to come closer and when I did, I felt a heat that I couldn't ignore. How could I keep penalizing the man I loved because someone else did something horrible to me? Looking at Maxwell sitting on the stool in front of the keyboard, wearing nothing but a pair of marled jogger sweatpants from Aeropostale, his pecan tan skin seemed to glisten and his well-defined chest had me thinking of all the things we use to do. I sat there close to him and he began to play another song and sing sweetly as he looked directly into my eyes. "Say love, When I look into your eyes, I get butterflies, Almost every time, Say, hey love, Every time we meet, Girl I get so weak, I can't even speak, Oh no, I wish you could be here all the time, Cause baby you belong by my side, What more can I say, I'm always thinking of you, You make it so easy to love you, Baby, baby, bae, It's never too hard to, Revolve my world around you, You make it so easy to love you." Again my eyes filled with tears listening to the lyrics. Maxwell had an amazing gift, and I was glad he thought enough of me to share it. When he stopped singing and looked toward me again, he had a look of concern on his face. "Baby, what's wrong?" he asked as he wiped a tear from my eye. "I've never experienced anyone like you, Max." I looked into his eyes and it felt as if he could see my heart; in the same moment, I believed that he was showing me his. "Make love to me," I added in a low voice. I could tell he was caught completely off guard. "Are you sure?" he asked. "I don't want you to think that's what this night was for." "Make love to me, Maxwell," I repeated, using more force as I placed both hands on his cheeks and brought his lips to mine. "Make love to me ...right here." I gave him a stare to let him know there was no reason to ask again. He began kissing me with a passion I'd forgotten existed. He looked into my eyes again and then paused. "Wait," he said as he turned to his iPod deck to replay the song he had just been singing, 'Easy to Love You' by Novel. He pulled my body close to his own and kissed me slow and deep. "Take off your clothes," he instructed. I did as I was told. He picked me up and laid me on the futon that sat in the corner of his music room. He trailed soft slow kisses down my stomach until he reached my love and in no time, his tongue was inside. His gentle teasing tongue sent chills down my spine as he made slow soft circles, brushing against my clit every now and then. He made sounds like he hadn't had dessert in weeks and my apple pie was the best thing on the menu. It turned me on every time I heard him say 'ummm'. "I want you," I whispered just as I was nearing my orgasm, but my breathing had changed so Maxwell ignored me. He rolled his tongue on my spot and flicked it with the fervor of a vibrator, and I began to ride my orgasmic wave like a pro surfer. "Oh. My. God!" I cried out. Maxwell lifted himself from between my thighs and gave me a look that said it wasn't over yet. He kissed me so I could taste the way my juices had adorned his pillow soft lips and I licked around them to turn him on even more. He slowly inserted himself inside, closing his eyes as he allowed my body to suck him in, as if it had been awaiting his return. "Damn, Shanice," he said as he began to work himself in and out of me slowly. I moved my hips to match his rhythm. Maxwell made love to me like this was the last time and I could feel his heart in every thrust. I could tell he didn't want to hurt me, as every move was slow and deep, but what he didn't know was that I had never experienced a more sensual moment. "Shanice?" he whispered. "Yes?" "Have my baby." I was caught off guard but welcomed the words he had just spoken. "Give me your seed," I replied, allowing him to cum long and hard with no regrets. Maxwell was everything to me, and I prayed that I was the same to him.

*****

"No, that's ugly. Our nephew is not about to be crawling around here looking unloved all because you don't know how to shop for a boy," Tameka said as she snatched the outfit I held up for her right out of my hand. "I'm paying though," I responded with a smile and as much patience as I could muster, knowing she meant well and was excited about the shopping trip. "No, actually Max is paying and I'm not about to let you waste that man's money," she quipped as she hung the outfit back on the rack. "Now this is cute!" She held up a Carter's outfit with a cute little blue and white plaid shirt and some khaki pants. "Yeah it's cute but $22.00? He's going to grow out of it ... like tomorrow," I joked as I noticed the price tag. "And your point is?" she asked, holding her manicured hands up in mock confusion. I hated shopping with Tameka, and hated her knowing that we were spending someone else's money. I told her I wanted to go grab some things for Elijah and when she came by to pick me up, Maxwell made the mistake of handing over his debit card in front of her. "My point is that I'm not trying to go crazy in this store just because it's Max's money," I responded as I took the outfit from her hand and hung it up. "Look, here's a clearance rack." She sucked her teeth and followed me to the clearance racks where we picked up over twenty items and spent only $80.00. We purchased several outfits he could wear now and some more things he would soon grow into. I also knew this was not the last time Max and I would be shopping for him. He was my youngest nephew, but Tameka's first so I knew she was real excited but after buying for all three of Tameka's kids the excitement for me had worn off years ago. We threw the bags in the trunk and headed to Sharon's. "Hey," Dan said with a slight hesitation as he opened Sharon's door. "Hey," I said dryly, standing in the doorway. Tameka didn't speak at all as she quickly brushed past Dan as if he hadn't been standing there. "Come in," he sighed as he rolled his eyes, extending his arm. Sharon and the baby were on the couch and the little one looked so peaceful. Dan's daughter, Danielle, was sitting at the opposite end of the couch, looking a little upset. "Hey, pretty girl," Tameka crooned, speaking to Danielle with her sweetest smile. "Hey," the little girl replied. "Are you happy to have a baby brother?" Tameka asked. The little girl shrugged. "Yeah, she's happy," Dan answered as he picked Danielle up and sat her on his lap. "I wish someone would have asked you," Tameka challenged, her words filled with attitude. "Stop it," I scolded, glaring at my sister, hoping the look I'd shot her would settle the tension she was creating, but it was apparent by the look on her face that Tameka had more to say. "What?" she said indignantly, looking at me and Sharon. "Am I seriously the only one who feels like his lying ass shouldn't be here?" "Look, if you're going to disrespect me, you can leave," Dan said in an effort to defend himself. "Boy, you can't put me out of nothing my sister is paying for," she replied as she rolled her eyes at him. Sharon finally spoke up. "Okay, can the two of you stop? If you're here to see the baby, please do ...but I don't want any more drama." I handed her the bag with all of the clothes that we'd just purchased and Sharon's face lit up. "Thanks, Shann--," she paused as she stopped herself from calling me Shannie. "Shanice, I really appreciate it." "No problem," I replied kindly. "And you can call me Shannie." I gave her my warmest smile in an effort to show her all was forgiven, hoping the gesture would ease the awkwardness of the moment. "Can you tell Maxwell that I'm really sorry for all this?" she asked, looking down. "No, I can't. I don't believe in smoothing things over for grown folks. When you feel like you can talk to him, you can apologize yourself." I was being honest. "Okay," she responded quietly. "As long as it's okay with you that I call." "It is fine," I assured her. "I trust him completely." I made it very clear that I was on his side. I couldn't help but notice the look on Dan's face as we talked about Max, and I almost felt bad for him ...almost. Tameka's silence meant she was somewhat entertained by his obvious discomfort too, although her body language suggested she was more than ready to leave. "Well, we're going to go," I announced. "We have an appointment at David's Bridal and I don't want to be late." I purposely threw in the location, not so much to offend Sharon but to ruffle Dan's feathers. I knew it had because he rolled his eyes as soon as the words left my lips. "Okay, Shannie. Thank y'all so much for the baby stuff," Sharon smiled. "Yeah, thanks," Dan said dryly. "Whatever," Tameka said to him as we walked toward the door. "Aye, Shanice... wait up. I have to ask you something." Dan put his daughter down and hurried toward the door behind us. Tameka stood there as if he was talking to her. "Can I ask you in private?" "No," Tameka challenged him with one hand on her hip. "Okay," he sighed. "Don't worry about it." He returned to his spot on the couch and we turned to leave. I made a mental note to ask him what it was he wanted next visit, but Tameka wasn't about to allow Dan to speak privately or have any alone time with me.

Chapter 6

MAXWELL

"You're a spoiled ass dude," Jackson said as he entered my office, shutting the door behind him. "I didn't ask for your judgment, bruh," I defended myself as I gave him a cold hard stare. "So they tell you that you're going to Fort Drum and you purposely fail two PT to test to get chaptered out?" He looked very disappointed but I didn't really care. If he was really my friend, he'd still be in my corner, even after all this was said and done, regardless of if he agreed with my decision or not. "Look Jack, I'm about to get married soon and we're trying to start a family," I explained to him, knowing I didn't have to. "Also, I don't want to move my wife and kids away from my mother. She's my only family. I had a great run, but I'm done." "Start a family? Are you sure you're ready for that, man? You know, I have six kids with five different baby mamas. That baby shit ain't all it's cracked up to be ...and my wife? She's more like a warden," he complained, as he normally did. "Well, I welcome the warden as long as it's Shanice, and I'm not about to have thirteen baby mamas. I'm going to have one, so chill," I laughed at him, shaking my head. Jackson was in his late thirties but swore he was twenty-one. His wife, Jasmine, was a really good woman. She had to be to put up with him and all his baby mamas. He had one child with her and she stood by him to no end. I wished like hell Shanice would do the same for me, especially after figuring out that I wouldn't lie to her like Dan had. "You laughing man," he argued, "but I'm serious. I hope you're ready to have another mother 'cause that's how these damn women are. They're cool when you're dating ...but as soon as you say 'I do', you will wish you'da said 'I don't'. He walked out of my office shaking his head, and I was doing the same. Jackson was quick to talk that shit but he wouldn't leave Jasmine if his life depended on it. I returned to the house later than normal. I'd been out with Rowland, consoling him with conversation and drinks because he'd found out that his evil sister, La'Draysha, has breast cancer. I was sympathetic to his feelings, but I couldn't help but think that she deserved it, considering all the misery she'd caused in other peoples' lives. I could hear the smooth sound of Charlie Parker throughout the house as I made my way to Shanice's favorite spot, the veranda. I stepped outside and immediately recognized the piece she was listening to, 'If I Should Lose You'. Shanice still hadn't noticed my presence as she sipped her dry martini and stared out across the backyard, seeming to be in a trance-like state. She had candles lit to provide light across the veranda and into the darkness of the evening, and even though I could tell she was sad, her beauty emanated as brightly as those candles' flames. Looking at her caramel complexion in the candlelight as the flame danced and shined in the night left me at a loss for words. Her hair was pulled up into a messy bun and her lips were pouty and kissable, though I knew this was not the moment in which she would want to be kissed. She wore a tank top and a pair of my Nike basketball shorts. There was nothing on her pedicured feet. After standing there for several moments, drinking every inch of her in, I finally spoke, "Hey, beautiful." Shanice turned my way and smiled slightly, but there was no twinkle in her eyes that said she was happy to see me tonight. "Hey, you," she said softly. "Why the sad song?" I asked, trying to find out what was on her mind and hopefully make her feel better by chasing her sadness and worries away. "I don't know," she mused, thinking about my question. "Charlie just understands how I'm feeling right now." "What's going on?" I asked, lifting a brow. I wanted to know what was on her mind, but that look... I'd seen that expression before and it worried me. "I love you Max ...and I love the way you love me but," she began. Out of impulse, I looked away for a moment. When a person says I love you but, the results are never good. "Don't do that, Maxwell," Shanice said before continuing. "I just don't feel like I deserve you. I went back to Dan after everything with you and Sharon ...and I don't even really know why. I'm confused, Max." "Confused about what?" I couldn't see where she was going with this conversation, but already it was leaving a bad taste in my mouth. My stomach knotted up as I listened to her words as she continued to speak. "I don't know if what we have is real or if it's just a reaction to my situation with Dan. I never took any time to breath, to heal." Tears rolled down her cheeks as she spoke, and I could feel my heart sinking in my chest. "So Shannie," I said reluctantly, "what are you really saying to me?" She slid the engagement ring off of her finger and placed it in my hand. "I need time," she answered, looking down. I was in complete shock and didn't know what I should be saying. "Are you really doing this again?" I asked. "It's not because I don't love you, Maxwell," Shanice sighed. I could feel emotion welling up in my throat and my heart beating in my neck as I became angry. "I just let go of my career for stability with you, and you keep playing these damn games!" I challenged her, raising my voice. I couldn't hold my temper. "You'll give Dan chance after chance but I keep getting used for the fucking moment." "That's not true," she said through tears as I turned my back toward her. It must have dawned on her what I'd just said as I was walking away because she spoke again. "You let go of your career?" "It doesn't matter," I said softly, starting to calm my temper a bit. This was it for me. I wasn't going to allow Shanice to hurt me again.

Chapter 7

DANDRIDGE

"**P**ills and potions, We're overdosing, I'm angry, but I still love you, Pills and potions, We're overdosing, Can't stand it, but I still love you." "Can you please let Nicki sing it?" I heard Sharon yell over the music. I'd just purchased Nicki Minaj's album, 'The Pinkprint', on iTunes and decided to give it a listen as I cleaned up Sharon's condo. "I'm sorry. Did I wake you and Elijah?" I asked as I lowered my Beats by Dre studio headphones from my ears. "No, he's still asleep," she answered with a smile. "I never pictured you as the domestic type." She pointed at the vacuum cleaner I'd been pushing around all morning. "I can't live in a dirty house," I said. "Live?" she questioned, instantly raising one of her eyebrows. "You know what I mean, stay, visit ...all that," I shrugged, struggling for words to define the situation, or perhaps a term that Sharon would approve of. Truth is, while I tried making things sound good for her, I really did mean live. I couldn't take my eyes off of her as she smiled at me. "Okay, Dan." She walked past me and into the kitchen. I watched as she poured herself a glass of orange juice, and then stood by the sink so she could put her cup in as soon as she was finished. She was wearing a pink satin slip that was much like a lot of the lingerie I'd seen her in over the past couple of weeks. She was so sexy. I didn't know how Max was able to turn her down. I walked into the kitchen and stood as close to her as possible, trying not to make the moment awkward or uncomfortable. "So do you always walk around the house in lingerie, or is this something you've started since I got here?" I asked playfully. "Of course it's all for you, Dan," she quipped as she rolled her eyes playfully and stepped around me. "I bet it is," I said as I gently grabbed her arm and turned her toward me. She looked up into my eyes and I immediately kissed her before she had time to process the moment. Her lips were so soft pressed against mine, and I felt something inside that I'd never felt with Shanice or Cecelia. It felt like an electric bolt had passed through my body and ignited everything within me. "What are you doing?" Sharon demanded as her hands found my chest and pushed me away. I was somewhat surprised that she had ended the kiss and resisted my advances so easily. I opened my mouth but the words wouldn't come. I wanted to defend myself but I had no explanation for my actions or advances. I was also worried that I might say the wrong thing and end my chances with Sharon for good. "I can't go there with you, Dan," Sharon mumbled, visibly upset. "I'm sorry... you really should leave." She walked out of the kitchen and down the hallway which led to her bedroom. I was on her heels, determined this was not the end of our conversation. "Leave? Why?" I asked in a tone I wasn't proud of. "I want to be here with you and my son." I sounded like a little bitch, begging to stay. "You can come back to visit him later," she sighed sadly, turning away from me, "but right now, you need to go." I lowered my head in defeat. Sharon and I had a connection, but I didn't know how long she would fight the feelings I was almost sure she felt for me.

*****

"Your mother did what?" my father questioned,

visibly shocked and unsure if he had heard the news correctly. "Yeah, she married that bastard," I stewed, shaking my head slightly as I took a sip of my Bud Light Platinum. "Did you tell your mother how he treated you when you approached him about being your dad?" he countered nervously, placing his can on the coaster and popping his knuckles. It was a habit, something he always did whenever he was upset about mom or one of us kids. "Nope, I'm pretty much done with them both," I answered with all the resolve I could muster, taking another long drink. "He's just as messed up as she is." My father shook his head and took a sip of his beer too. I was thankful that he didn't try to convince me otherwise. "Why didn't she call and tell me about the cancer?" he asked, wiping the sweat from his can and drying his hand down the side of his leg. "I honestly thought that she and I were a little bit better than this ...and that she'd at least tell me something that important." "Why tell you when she has Jamie?" I asked. Instantly regretting the words as soon as they had left my lips, I made a face to show my disgust. I was angry with my mother but I had no reason to get smart with my father. "Well, it's her life," he answered quietly, his face unchanging as he nonchalantly took a larger swig of beer from the can this time. I wondered how much the news of my mother's cancer was really bothering him. "What little bit she has left," I mumbled, a little surprised by my own callousness but I shrugged it off. I owed my mother no sympathy. In fact, I was fairly certain karma was the blame for her sudden decline in health. You can only be a vile evil wench for so long before all of those wrongdoings start to catch up with you. "Don't do that, son. You and your sisters need to spend as much time with your mother as possible before she dies, if that's even the case." He lowered his voice as the bartender walked past, collecting the empty cans from our last round. "Do you know what stage the cancer is in?" "No sir," I answered meekly. "Hopefully, it's stage four." I took another swig of my beer, refusing to look my father's way because I already knew the look he was giving me. "Forgive her, son. What's done is done," he pleaded gently as he placed a hand on my shoulder. "Can't nobody change the past …only the future can be rewritten." I didn't respond. I was tired of talking about my mother. She wasn't the reason I'd invited him for a couple of cold ones anyway. "But what I really came to see you about is... I have feelings for Sharon," I announced, not sure how he would react. "Out of this whole fucked up situation, she's bringing the one thing out of me that nobody else could." I turned my barstool so I could study his face, looking for some clues as to how he would respond to the declaration of my newfound love. "And what's that?" he asked, sounding a bit defeated as he set his beer can on the cardboard coaster, pushing the ashtray farther away. I had hoped for a little more enthusiasm from my father. "The truth," I answered him matter of factly. Because I can't lie to her, I've been forced to be honest with other people too ...because the truth includes her," I explained, thinking that I must sound somewhat ridiculous to my dad, but he must have understood. "What about Shanice?" he asked, swishing the last couple of gulps around, inside the aluminum can. "What about her?" My dad let out a slight laugh. "How does she feel about you wanting to be with her sister?" "She's engaged to the closest thing I had to a brother, dad... my best friend. I could care less how she feels." I was being honest. Shanice was the furthest thing from my mind these days. When I had tried to ask Shanice if I could pursue Sharon with her blessings, Tameka wouldn't excuse herself long enough for me to have a private moment with her. In that instant, I just chalked the whole thing up to water under the bridge and decided to move forward without her blessing. "Shanice has been through a lot, thanks to you and your mother," he said as if I needed to be reminded of my transgressions. "She deserves to hear this from you before it gets too deep." My father dropped a couple of twenties on the bar and walked out, leaving me with my beer and my thoughts.

Chapter 8

LA'DRAYSHA

I sat in doctors office, hooked up to the machine that fed the chemo into my body. Exhausted and struggling to stay awake, I looked around at the other women sitting around me. They appeared to be just as drained and sick as I was. "Do you need anything?" Tina asked. She, Rowland and Jamie had all been taking turns, transporting me to and from chemo. "No, I'm fine," I smiled weakly, thankful for her kindness. "Just bring my pen and notebook." I'd been carrying that notebook around since my diagnosis, writing letters that would be given to my kids once I passed away. Tina and Rowland had both been praying that God would heal my body, but I didn't see how prayer was going to change my situation now. I was a goner and everyone knew it. The chemo hadn't been helping any and I was still periodically seeing and talking to my mother because the cancer had spread through my body and into my brain, causing frequent hallucinations. It felt as if I was stuck in an episode of Grey's Anatomy. I decided it was time to write a letter for Dan. I needed to apologize to him for the way I always took control of his life and made him feel as though he couldn't make his own choices. I needed him to understand that I tried to stop Frankie from raping Shanice but the deed had already been done, and that I just wanted him to be happy. I'd spoken to Jamie several times about establishing a relationship with Dan but he always refused my request, thinking it was just too late for a father and son relationship now. My only wish was that I would be able to bring my family together before my life ended. I wanted to fix at least one thing that I had broken over the years.

*****

"Are you sure you're up to this?" Tina asked as we walked through the mall. I smiled and shrugged my shoulders. "If I start looking weak, just grab me a wheel chair," I joked. "That's not funny, Draysha," she scolded me. I could see that she was truly worried about my lack of strength. "Girl, we are just picking up a few things for my grandbabies," I reassured, hoping she would lighten up a little and have some fun with me today. "Shouldn't take too long..." She stepped into JC Penney's and I immediately turned my nose up. "You always looking for a sale." I looked at Tina like she knew better than to go into JC Penny. "Oh my God... even Cancer won't humble you!" She covered her mouth as soon as the words had escaped, upset for the way her words had surely sounded. "Let's go to Nordstrom's." "Okay," she agreed reluctantly, rolling her eyes to further remind me that she hated shopping in places like that. Shopping at Nordstrom's meant we had to walk all the way to the other end of the mall but I was determined to spend the rest of my energy on some darling new duds for my grands. I was the first to notice Shanice walking toward the door with some man ...and it wasn't Maxwell. "Tee," I hissed as a pinched a handful of her blazer to pull her within earshot of my raspy whisper. "Look!" Tina turned toward the door but didn't seem surprised at the sight. Instead, my friend began to hurry toward them. "Hey, Shanice!" Tina called out with a wave, capturing

Shanice's attention from across the crowded store on her first attempt. "Miss Taylor," Shanice smiled sweetly, although I thought she looked a bit nervous. "Hi." The man stood quietly by her side, seemingly absorbed in a nearby display. He was dressed well. His silence taunted me even more than her lack of manners. "Who's your friend?" I asked sweetly, like it was my business. To hell with introductions, I thought. She looked at me and rolled her eyes. I continued to smile, but I was surprised they didn't get stuck in the back of her head as hard as she rolled them. "This is Reagan," Shanice began. "Reagan, this is Miss Taylor." She purposely acted as if I wasn't the one who asked for an introduction. "That's a very feminine name," I said before Tina could respond. Shanice still ignored me and so did her friend. "We saw you two and decided to come over and speak," Tina spoke quickly, trying to ease the tension. "We'll let you two get back to your day." Shanice looked as if she had been caught doing something wrong as she said good-bye and walked away. "I knew that child was triflin'. That was odd," I mused. "I'm definitely going to call Maxwell." Tina watched the two of them disappear through the double glass doors and exit the shopping mall. We continued onward with our journey to the baby

Chapter 9

MAXWELL

"'m sure it was nothing," I sighed as I spoke to my mom about Shanice. I wasn't sure what to think. "Well, she looked real guilty," my mom replied, justifying her suspicions. "You know I like Shanice, but we both know she hasn't been the best when it comes to good judgment." "Well ma, we all make mistakes." I took up for her, just as I always did when ma was worried about me. "Yeah but you need to stop letting her make mistakes with your heart, son," ma said worriedly. "You deserve so much better." I didn't like being the source of my mother's stress and worrying. "I know, ma," I answered reassuringly as I looked up to see Shanice enter the living room. "She won't hurt me again," I continued. "I promise." I looked in her direction, not bothering to hide the fact that we were talking about her. "If you say so," my mother sighed, sensing by my tone that Shanice was within earshot and I was ready to end the conversation. "I love you, Maxwell." "I love you too, ma," I responded kindly. "I'll be over there tomorrow." "Reagan, huh?" I said accusingly, hanging up the phone just as Shanice was about to walk away. "He's just a friend, Max. We worked together at Christine's." I laughed slightly before responding. "No need to explain to me, Miss I-need-time." I shook my head as I realized that I couldn't deal with history repeating itself once again. "I'm not letting you or your actions take me down the path it did the last time," I added, verbalizing my thoughts. "Nobody said they had to," she snapped at me. "You're a real piece of work, man. Do me a favor... be out of my house by the end of the month," I fired back at her. I was pissed. "Max, that's only a week and a half," she pleaded with fear in her eyes. "Well, maybe you should've dumped me on the first," I yelled back to her as I sauntered toward my bedroom, not giving Shanice the chance to say anything else. I was tired of her toying with me. It was time that I let her go once and for all, and figure out my own life.

*****

I sat at my keyboard silently for a little while, not knowing what I should play. I was hurting but kept telling myself not to worry about Shanice. I was there for her when she needed someone, every time... but she kept leaving me. How could that girl be so blinded that she could not see that I was the man she deserved? She clearly knew that I was the one she needed because every time the chips were down, I was the first person she ran to. "Why you wanna do this to me, We supposed to get married, Did you ever stop to think at all, This would tear a hole in me, Did ever even care at all, that I'd be questioning, Will I ever love again, Will I ever trust again, Will I ever feel again, The kind of love that I felt for her, Until then, I'll just be broken man I found myself playing Anthony Hamilton's 'Broken Man' and a tear rolled down my cheek as I sang the words. Shanice would never know how bad she'd hurt me. She was so consumed with herself and how everyone made her feel that she didn't think about the feelings of others. I sat there wanting to hate her, but I loved her so much. I looked in mirror, giving myself a thorough once over. I looked good. I was wearing a pair of red chinos with a light jean button down and a pair of round toe cognac Dwang loafers I'd recently purchased from Aldo. I put a pair of square diamond stud earrings in each ear, sprayed on some Polo Double Black and headed for the door, making sure to walk through the kitchen when I heard Shanice in there. I wanted her to see how good I looked and smelled on my way out the door. I was going to Jazz 101 Lounge, a new 25 and up Jazz club located in downtown Raleigh. Hip hop clubs weren't really my thing and I'd rather not party with the 18 or 21 and up crowds because they didn't know how to act. I was in the mood for a good chill night, a night that would hopefully take my mind and emotions off of Shanice.

Chapter 10

SHANICE

Maxwell was being such an ass. He walked into the kitchen looking as fine as ever, wearing the Polo Double Black cologne I'd given him when he graduated from his master's program. He was normally a homebody so I was curious to know where he was going but I bit my tongue, refusing to ask. I decided to use the time Max was gone to start packing my things. I hadn't been there two months and already I was leaving again, but this time because I needed time and space. I knew Miss Taylor would immediately call to tell Max that she'd seen me leaving the mall with Reagan, but there really wasn't anything to tell ...and now I was homeless because of Maxwell's jealousy. "I have to stop depending on these niggas," I said aloud as a disclaimer to myself. "Don't move in with another man unless he's your husband." I continued to talk to myself. By the time I finished packing, I was exhausted and as much as I wanted to leave for Tameka's tonight, I didn't feel like taking the drive across town. Instead, I decided to put my bags in the car and leave first thing in the morning. "Max, you are just as silly as I remembered," crooned a female voice, which was followed by some giggling. I turned over to see the clock on the nightstand which read 3:45 a.m. I slowly eased the door knob as far left as it would go and carefully opened the door so they wouldn't hear me. I tiptoed down the hall until I was just close enough to overhear the conversation being held between the two of them. "Yeah I bet," he said. "So how is um... what's his name? You know... the dude you cheated on me with." Max sounded like he was still holding a grudge and that's when I knew he was talking to none other than Kimberly Hill, his first love. "I guess he's doing okay. There's probably a lot of truth to the saying 'you'll lose them the same way you got them' because I returned home from a visit with my mother before she passed, and found my soon-to-be husband in bed with someone else," she admitted. "I'm sorry," was Maxwell's response and it sounded genuine, which thoroughly pissed me off. How could he feel sorry for the woman who cheated on him during his deployment, but not feel sorry enough for me to at least give me time to find another place to stay? 'That bastard,' I scowled quietly, mouthing the words. "Well you know I never stopped thinking about you," I heard him say. "Oh, really? How many bitches did you call me when I came to mind," she laughed sweetly. "I would never call you anything, outside of your name. I loved you." This conversation was getting worse and worse by the minute, and I could feel my heart shrinking inside my chest. "So, even after all these years, you still think the best of me?" The room fell silent for a minute and when he answered, my legs grew weak and I nearly lost my footing. "I could never think the worst of you. We were young but you stayed on my mind, even when I thought I was in love with other women." I turned and walked back to my room, leaning against the wall for support. I couldn't stand to listen to their conversation anymore. Maxwell was a dog just like all the other men in the world, and I was thankful that I'd dropped his lying, scheming ass before making the biggest mistake of my life. I opened the door to my room and fell face first onto the bed in tears. I had only wanted some time to be sure and I thought that, if anyone would understand that, it would be Max. We hadn't been over for a full week yet and here he was, already trying to see what was up with Kim or as he so eloquently put it, 'the woman who stayed on his mind even when he thought he was in love'. I heard the sound of the keyboard as Maxwell started singing Fantasia's Barrino's version of 'You Were Always on My Mind'. My thoughts traveled back to the night we made love and he asked me to have his baby. Now he was pulling that same smooth 'let me sing to you' act for her. Men never changed their game up …they just change the players.

*****

"Hello?" Sharon answered the phone sleepily. "I'm sorry for calling so early, Sharon, but I really need a place to stay until I can find something. Is it possible for me to crash at your place?" She was certainly the last person I ever thought I'd be asking for a favor. "I'm sorry, Shannie, but no." Her voice trembled a little as she spoke, like she afraid to turn me away. "Thanks anyway." I was about to hang up when I heard Dan's voice in the background. "Ey bae, how do you like your steak cooked?" he asked her. "Medium," was the last thing I heard her say before the call was disconnected. "What the fuck is wrong with everybody?" I yelled. Dan and Sharon? How could he go running to my sister after being with me for eleven years? This day couldn't possibly get any worse I thought. I got into my car and headed to the last place I ever thought I'd stay again. "So you messed up with the only man that wanted to do you right, neither one of your sisters want you at their place, you haven't spoken to me in weeks, but now that you need a place to lay yo' head and wash yo' ass, you're at my house?" my grandmother asked, deciding to point out all the obvious. Her expression softened a bit as she spoke again. "You can stay ...but you sleeping on the couch," she sighed heavily. "You know yo' mama living here now, too." I rolled my eyes and said thank you through my teeth. My grandmother's house was not my idea of a good time ...that was for sure. I was still upset with her about the situation that had occurred with Dan's mom, and how she'd lied to me and Tameka for twenty-six-years, and still hadn't made a real effort to apologize. She'd left a voicemail on my phone, talking about how terribly ungrateful I was after she had taken me in and how my biggest problem was that I was spoiled. I shook my head and placed my bags in the living room deciding to call Meka and have meet me to talk and drink. "I'm sorry I couldn't let you stay with me, Shannie, but you know it's already hard, being that I live in that little two bedroom piece of apartment. I'm on the couch at my own damn house so your nieces can share a room and your nephew has a room alone," she explained as we sat at our favorite bar and had drinks. "It's cool, Meka," I replied. "I really do understand." I threw back a very potent jello shot, hoping the liquor would numb the pain a little. She wore a confused look on her face as she asked, "So why are you no longer staying with Max?" "We broke up." I motioned for the bartender to bring me another shot. I loved those one dollar jello shots. "Again?" she asked in shock as she placed her drink emphatically down on the bar. "For what reason this time?" "I told him that I needed time to heal, and to be by myself for a while," I said, holding my voice low and steady. "So I could be sure... and he took that as go out and fuck Kimberly Hill." "Kim Hill... the one from high school?" she asked in amazement. "One and the same," I replied. Tameka's eyes looked as if they were about to pop out of their sockets. "Hold on… the one who cheated on him when he was overseas doing a deed for our country?" She was having a hard time making sense of all that had happened. I was glad to not be the only one blown away by Maxwell's actions. "That would be the one," I answered, pursing my lips and nodding my head. "Shut yo' mouth and stop these lies, Shannie!" She threw back a shot before asking another question. "How you know he had sex with her?" "I heard it! He's so disrespectful! He knew I was still in the house and she was loud but hell, she had reason to be." "Damn, big sis. You just let that girl come in and take your good wood like that?" she asked as she shook her head at me. "Ey, bartender! Bring four more shots of Tequila 1800." I was on board with that. "Okay, so what happened when you called Sharon?" "Dandridge was cooking for her," I mumbled, shaking my head as I glanced at Tameka with a look that said 'yeah, that's right' and she started laughing. "What's so funny?" "You're always going on and on about how I have three baby daddys, and that I need to make better relationship choices…" "You do!" I cut her off. "Bye Felicia!" she interrupted me, holding up her hand to stop me from saying anything more. "Shannie, you have literally allowed your life to get away from you, and you have the nerve to not only judge me but give me advice? We can both agree that Dan wasn't shit but now he's at our sister's house cooking and shit. He never even made your ass a bowl of cereal." She stopped talking to quickly down her tequila shot before continuing. "Then there's Maxwell, who was actually great for you ...amazing even, and now he's back with his no good ex because you're still in love with Dan!" she accused as she laughed some more. "Heal my ass! You just want the nigga that's hittin' your little sister." Before I knew it, I'd slapped the tequila out of Tameka's mouth. She looked at me with a smile on her face. "It's funny," she spoke to me again. "Dan's mom isn't even working against you anymore and you're managing to lose everything ...all by yourself. Bye, Shannie, and don't bother calling me. Find someone else to share all the ridiculous details about your fucked ass love life with." She stormed out of the bar and one of the security guards followed her. "Baby daddy number four," I mumbled to myself, drinking the last shot of tequila in front of me. I ordered a few more drinks before I finally called a cab. I had no idea where I was going because Betty Mae had given me a curfew and it was well past ten.

Chapter 11

DANDRIDGE

"**W**ow! This is really good! Where'd you learn how to cook?" Sharon asked and I kind of didn't want to answer. "You don't want to know," I responded as I stuck a piece of steak in my mouth. "Oh, Shanice must have taught you," she said as she lowered her head and started pushing her food around with her fork. "Not actually. I use to watch her sometimes and make mental notes of what I saw her doing," I explained, wanting to ease her mind. "Did you ever show her what you'd learned?" "Nah," I laughed. "I never cooked for her. I barely wanted to get up and hand her a fruit cup out of the fridge." I was surprised at how easy the truth rolled off my tongue, even when it didn't make me look very good. "That's not funny, Dan," Sharon pouted, her expression suddenly very serious. "I'm just saying... you bring out a different man in me, a man I don't even recognize. That's why I like you, Sharon." The color rose in her cheeks, visibly flattered by my compliment. "I felt bad telling my sister that she couldn't crash here," she said, confiding in me. "Well, that would have been awkward but if you want to call her and say you've changed your mind, I can stay in a hotel until she finds a place," I offered, secretly praying that she would decline. "No, no," she objected, turning down my offer. "She has Tameka and our grandmother. She should be fine." I flashed her one of my biggest smiles and continued to eat my food. I barely knew what to say to Sharon. I was just so happy she'd let me come back when I called to apologize for the kiss. Sharon spoke again, "I wonder what happened with her and Max though?" "Probably some petty shit they'll get over, but let's not talk about them," I urged the beautiful woman I was sharing a meal with, hoping to dismiss the conversation about my ex. I'd had enough talk of Shanice and I definitely didn't want to talk about Maxwell. "Well, what would you like to talk about?" "First of all, I want to know if you thought by putting on those sweats, it was going to make you less sexy?" She looked down at her ensemble and laughed. "Actually yes, that's exactly what I thought." "I think you're beautiful either way," I told her as I reached across the table and took her hands in mine. "Dan, I told you we can't." "Why can't we?" I asked. "We already have a son together, Sharon. We could have a family." I paused because I couldn't believe those words had just escaped my lips. "Dan, why are you playing with me?" she asked as she rolled her eyes. "I'm not!" I answered indignantly, trying to convince this girl that I truly cared for her. "I'm serious." She stared at me for what seemed like forever before she spoke, and I was afraid of what she might say. "My sister would hate me," Sharon sighed sadly. "But your future husband would love you until death, so what's worth more?" Again, I couldn't believe the words that were coming out of me. "Future husband?" she asked, her eyes open wide in disbelief. Clearly, this was not the Dandridge that she, or anyone else, had ever known. "Yeah, I mean one day," I clarified, not wanting to be too eager and scare her away. "I don't know, Dan." I looked at her so hard, I'm sure she felt like I was staring into her soul. "Let me make love you. Let me use my tongue in ways that will make you think you've seen God face to face. Let me go so deep inside of your warm juicy lips that you feel me touching your heart. Let me give you a part of me that I've never given to anybody," I urged. She closed her eyes as I spoke and I knew she was imagining what it would feel like, what emotions we would experience while physically entwined with one another. I stood and walked around the table where I leaned down and kissed her, all the while praying that she wouldn't pull away as she had done before. She kissed back and before I knew it, she'd slid her tongue into my mouth which let me know that she was ready to accept me. I started to slowly undressed her and that's when she stopped me. "What's wrong?" I asked. "I'm not ready," Sharon admitted, lowering her eyes as she continued. "I want you but I'm not ready to take it there yet. Can we just date and see where things go?" I wasn't used to a female asking me to wait for anything, but for Sharon, I felt it would be well worth it. "Yes baby, we can wait." I kissed her forehead and went back to my side of the table to continue the dinner I'd prepared for us.

Four Months Later...

"Ever has it been that love knows not its own depth until the hour of separation."

-Kahlil Gibran

Chapter 12

MAXWELL

"That feels amazing," I moaned softly as I closed my eyes while Kimberly massaged my back in the Jacuzzi tub, her beautiful brown legs wrapped around me as I leaned back onto her perfect breasts. "I'm glad you're enjoying it," she said, laughing sweetly. I began to sing. "I need you to wrap them chocolate legs 'round me So when I come home tonight You'll make everything alright When you come wrap them chocolate legs 'round me The memory of my day Will quickly just fade away When you come wrap them chocolate legs 'round me Please baby, wrap them chocolate legs 'round me." She used her free hand to tap me on my head. "Boy, you always singing," she jokingly accused. "You love it, though." "So what if I do?" she asked softly and I couldn't help but smile. I was in heaven with Kimberly and, although my thoughts would frequently take me to Shanice, I knew that I was in a better relationship. Over the past four months, Kim had really shown me a better and more mature person and I remembered all the reasons for loving her. She'd dedicated herself to Christ and barely communicated with other men, outside of her family. "Well, if you love my singing, you'll love this too," I teased as I pulled her hand around to feel my erection. "Oh will I?" she asked coyly. "You know you will. This is what Eric Benet' was talking about, girl." I turned to position myself between her legs. "Wrap them chocolate legs 'round me," I said as I brought our lips together passionately. She wrapped her legs around my waist tightly as I guided myself inside of her. The feeling of the water mixed with our love making had me on a cloud. She softly bit down on my lip as I thrust myself in and out, careful not to disconnect our bodies. "Oh baby," she whimpered. "You love it?" "Yes," she moaned. "Yes baby, I love it!" "How much do you love it?" I asked, leaning right to make sure I hit her spot time and time again. "More than you know, Max," she screamed. "Cum for me then," I dove as deep inside as I could and her body began to shake. She held onto me, trying to get me stop for a second but I continued as if she didn't need a break. I pumped myself in and out and began to increase the speed as I felt myself about to give way. "Kim, it's so good baby," I moaned, just as I released myself inside of her. She leaned forward, the weight of her body against my chest. I could feel her small erect nipples pressing into me as she struggled to catch her breath from the orgasms. "If you could cook, you'd be a prize," I joked, slapping her ass playfully. "I could say the same for you," she countered. "I make the best cup of ramen you ever ate. Girl, you better recognize," I smiled. I loved how playful things were with Kim and me, most of the time. The only thing I hated was her bossiness, but I was beginning to learn how to make her feel like she was in control even when she wasn't. It cut down on disagreements and made us both happy. "So you're out of the Army in a week, bae. What's next?" she asked. "Music, music, music," I told her, watching as she tied a towel around her slim body. The years had been good to Kim; she was far more beautiful than the girl I remembered. I followed her to the kitchen and watched as she poured water into the tea kettle. I loved having her here but we had yet to delve into our life goals or discuss the future. Kim was between jobs, though she'd gotten a degree in accounting, and I was getting ready to embark on my new journey with my music. "Have you given any thought to what I said?" she asked, looking over her shoulder as she retrieved her favorite mug from the cabinet and scooted the tea canister where she could peer inside as she searched for her favorite herbal fix. I rolled my eyes at her as she took the stool across from me and cupped her hands around the mug, taking a sip and acting as if we hadn't had this conversation several times before. My first instinct was to shrug it off without a response but my temperament wouldn't allow my silence. "Look, we've been down this road a million times. I've tried to be friends with Dan, more than once, and he stabbed me in my back so I'm cool," I sighed impatiently before softening my tone. She was just trying to help and I appreciated her support. "Jackson is the closest thing I have to a best friend ...outside of you." I explained again as I kissed her lips and poured the cereal I'd been holding. "Okay," Kim smiled softly, her eyes assuring me that she was sorry to have brought his name up in conversation again. "I just feel that, if you could forgive me, then maybe there was hope for Dan, too." She hopped off the barstool and headed toward the living room, leaving her mug on the counter. Out of habit, I took her mug to the sink with my cereal bowl and cleaned them both, collecting the used tea bag and my empty cereal box to toss in the trash. As my foot touched the pedal and the lid popped open, my heart skipped a beat. Surely my eyes were deceiving me. This had to be something else I thought as I reached into the trashcan and pulled out the small cardboard package. Its contents rattled inside when I shook the box. The pregnancy test slid into my hands when I opened the flap. Two lines... I watched enough commercials on television to know what that meant. My head was spinning. "Umm... bae, do you have something you need to tell me?" I asked, standing in the living room, looking somewhat like a zombie while waving the test like a small wand. "What?" Kim's eyes were focused on the television, which was normal when one of her shows was on. Most of them were nothing but nonsense ...the stuff that kills brain cells, I had told her once. "Kim!" I said her name with enough force that I startled her. She turned around abruptly and her eyes fell to the object in my hand. "I..." she paused, obviously unsure about what to say to me. "I was going to tell you, Maxwell. I promise you that I wasn't trying to hide this from you. I was just waiting for the perfect moment to give you the news ...and we haven't discussed kids so I was trying to see where your head was at when I found the right time to bring it up." She looked nervous and upset as she fidgeted in her seat, but I was furious. "You lied to me," I said evenly, through clenched teeth. I looked at her with a straight face but I was trying not to lose my temper or raise my voice. "I don't know why I took your lying ass back," I added as she began to cry but that wouldn't stop me from speaking my mind. "You said you were on birth control." If I was anything like Ike Turner, I'da hit her so hard …her ancestors would have felt it. "I didn't lie, Max," she retorted, drying her cheeks with an open hand as she stood up, finding her voice. "And I'm tired of you feeling like every time something doesn't go your way, it's because I'm a liar. I was on the pill but that weekend where you decided to whisk me away to Miami? Well, I missed three days because I didn't have my pills and we spent more time having sex than we did enjoying Miami." I could tell she was being honest, and I remembered surprising her with that Florida trip. We were definitely doing it like some jackrabbits that weekend. "I'm sorry, I was just..." I said as my voice trailed off. I started to give her an excuse about being caught off guard but decided against it. "I shouldn't have assumed anything. I apologize," I said softly as I stretched out my arms for her to come into my embrace. "I'm glad you're having my baby." "Really?" She looked up at me with tears in her eyes. The words sounded strange as I had said them to Kim. I had always imagined those words would be spoken to another woman, but I had given up on that hope months ago. It was time to stop looking for something that was never going to happen and embrace the present. "Yes, really," I answered, kissing the crown of her head softly as she rested her cheek against my chest. I couldn't believe I was going to be a father, for real this time but more so... I couldn't believe that it wasn't by Shanice.

Chapter 13

LA'DRAYSHA

"**I**f I wanted to change I would have done it by now, but what I have realized is that I am too old to change." –La'Draysha Harris "This has to stop! Stop talking to dead people!" Jamie was growing frustrated with me and the frequent visits I'd been having with my mother. "If I could, I would," I snapped as I rolled my eyes. Jamie was such a good man for taking care of me and staying by my side. He'd arranged everything with my lawyer regarding my will and we had planned my funeral together. I now had stage four cancer and the doctors were telling me that I could go today or five months from now, they really didn't know. I did the best I could to fight it because I wanted to at least be around for Christmas, but in reality, I knew there was a chance I'd be gone. "Hello." I answered my cell phone almost before it rang. "I'm glad you're happy, girl," I said to the female on the other end. "Anytime," I replied. "You deserve it. Bye," I rushed to get off of the phone. Everyone thought I'd given up on the Fuller family but I couldn't rest until I knew they were unhappy. My plans seemed to have worked before but I was told that Shanice and Betty Mae made up, and Betty Mae was living her life just as happy. I wanted that woman to be miserable, and I wanted Shanice to be miserable. I had almost spent my final days in jail because of that little bitch.

Six Months ago...

"Hi, I'm detective Smith. Are you La'Draysha Harris?" the very stunning female cop asked. "Yes, I am." I looked at her like she had the wrong address. It was 8:00 a.m. and I was still in my house coat. "We need you to put on some clothes and come to the station with us. We have some questions to ask you." She seemed to have an attitude. "Excuse me, officer?" Tina seemed have come out of nowhere but I should have known she was listening. She'd spent the night on my couch the previous night. "Would it be okay if you just questioned her here? She's battling cancer and is on a very tight schedule with her medications. Unless you're here to arrest her?" Tina was very polite but you could tell she was challenging the officer a little. "Oh no, we didn't come for an arrest, just a few questions. We can do it here." The detective and her partner stepped over the threshold. "Coffee?" Tina asked them politely, as if this were her house. "No, but tea would be awesome if you have any." "Tea coming right up," Tina smiled as she disappeared into the kitchen. I offered the detectives a seat. Smith pulled out a small recorder and jumped straight in. "Do you know a woman by the name of Shanice Fuller?" I lifted a brow, immediately realizing what this little meet and greet was about. "Yes, I do." "Do you know a man by the name of Frankie Curry?" "No, I do not," I lied. The detectives exchanged looks as she continued. "Well, we picked Mr. Curry up and, for a while, he wouldn't tell us what made him rape Shanice Fuller but when offered a sweet deal to testify against that person, it was funny that your name was the one he gave us." She looked into my eyes like she'd be able to find the lie. "Well, there must be another La'Draysha

Harris around here because I don't know anyone by that name." "He said you paid him to not only rape Shanice but you also wanted him to kill her." I couldn't believe that bastard had lied on me. "Kill her? Why would I want Shanice dead? My son is madly in love with her ...and I love her too," I added, telling another lie. Smith laughed a bit. "Okay, Mrs. Harris, but understand this," the officer said as she leaned close to my face. "If we find out you're lying, you'll be fighting cancer from behind prison walls." "If you don't get your hot ass breath out of my face, I'll be serving time for the beat down of Detective Smith," I responded coolly. "Are you threatening me?" "No ma'am," I smiled. "I'm making you a promise." She stood to leave. "Tell your maid I'll take a rain check on the tea," she said with a nod. "I've got a feeling I will be back for another visit." "Maid," I heard Tina repeat with attitude as she stood in the doorway to the living room, holding the glasses. "Goodbye, Detective ...and I am nobody's maid." Tina sat the glasses down and followed them to the door. As soon as the officers were off of the stoop, she shut and locked the door. I could see the storm in her eyes and knew in a moment, there would be more questions. "You hired someone to kill that girl?" Tina demanded. Her mouth was wide open, shocked at the thought of what she had heard. I peered out the window and across the lawn to make sure the police officers were gone before I answered her. "No," I whispered in an agitated hiss. "I paid him to rape her. I admit that, but I never said that I wanted her dead." I walked to my bedroom and picked up the phone I used to contact Frankie. I didn't know if he was in jail or not but he answered on the first ring. "What?" "I thought you were in jail." "I'm out on bond," he mumbled. "What do you want?" "Why did you lie to those people? I didn't tell you to kill anybody." I was livid. "Bitch, please!" he laughed. "You sent me a letter after you paid me, and told me to get rid of her." I had no idea what he was talking about; I didn't write any letter. "Stop telling them people you know me," I ordered as I hung up the phone. Tina was banging on my bedroom door but I didn't want to talk. I didn't feel like hearing about how wrong I was for having that girl raped, but I did write a nice little letter and would wait for the perfect time to send it off. Shanice wasn't going to put me behind bars if I had anything to say about it. Present Day... "Who was that on the phone?" Jamie asked. "Nobody," I shrugged, feigning disinterest in the matter. "I think they had the wrong number." He lifted his brow. "You're happy for someone who has the wrong number?" "The girl was talking and didn't give me a chance to say it was the wrong number so I told her I was happy for her ...said something about getting married and having a baby," I lied. "Do you need your notepad?" he asked, still shaking his head as he held up the notebook I was writing my letters in. "No, I think all of my letters are complete," I replied thoughtfully. "Just put that in a safe place until the end." The end, whenever that was. It sounded so terrible but I would be ready. I sat upright in the bed and positioned my pillows, thinking about how none of my kids had contacted me since I told them about the cancer. Tina said Dan was dating Sharon now and he seemed grateful for the things I sent over. Cecelia came to visit me with Danielle and a two month old Dayna at least once a week which made me happy. I really hated that Dan left that girl but she seemed to be handling it fine, except on the few occasions where she'd vent to me about missing him. "Why don't you tell them you've changed and that you're sorry?" she asked me during her last visit as we discussed the fact that I hadn't seen any of them. "If I wanted to change, I would have done it by now," I explained, "but one thing I have realized is that I'm too old to change."

Chapter 14

SHANICE

"You still haven't talked to Max," Reagan asked as he sipped his beer, focusing on what seemed to be a very intense game of NBA 2k on his XBOX One. He and I had decided to become roommates after only one week of me staying with grandmother. I was afraid to live alone and his mom wanted him out of her house so it seemed to be the perfect situation. "Talked to him for what?" I sighed. "He made his choice." I was so tired of discussing Maxwell with everybody. They all acted like I didn't have a life outside of that man. "But you also made a choice for him," he replied, without looking away from his game, "one that he should have been included in. If my girl did some shit like that, I think I would have tried to kill her." "Well, I'm not his girl." "But that was that man's baby. Y'all females kill me making choices for other people. You broke things off with him and aborted his child because you mad he moved on," he murmured, shaking his head. "That's bullshit." Reagan was always upsetting himself by bring up the subject. "Let's change the subject," I pleaded, hoping he would let it go. I couldn't bear to think about the past today. He shook his head. "I don't understand why you don't just tell him about the letter that lady sent you. You should have told Max and the two of you gone to the police. Are you so scared of this woman's threats that would just let her control your life though?" I lowered my head because the answer to his question was yes. I actually was that afraid of Miss Harris and felt that Reagan shouldn't be so hard on me. He had no idea what this lady was capable of. "You don't know her, okay? She would have gotten locked up and still found some type of way to make good on her threat. I would rather just leave well enough alone and move forward with my life," I sighed, knowing this wasn't the first time I had explained myself to my new roommate. "Well, if you're moving forward," he questioned, "why haven't you thrown the letter away? You need a constant reminder of why you're not with ol' boy?" "Oh, now he's ol' boy? A few minutes ago, you knew his name," I challenged with a laugh. "I'm just saying if you're really set on not being with that man, get rid of the letter and live your life. You've been held up in this apartment for months now, only leaving to go to work and the grocery store. Get out and meet somebody," he urged. "I mean... I would say me, but I have a girl and I kind of love her." Reagan winked and I had to laugh. "I'm glad you love her!" I picked up one of the throw pillows and threw it him. I couldn't stay upset because I knew Reagan was trying to be my friend. I walked into the kitchen and retrieved the letter that La'Draysha had sent me four months ago. I stood there, read it one last time. Shanice, I hope this letter finds you doing well. I know you went to the police about your little rape episode. That was a bad idea, so here's what you're going to do. You're going to go to the police and drop your little case completely. Tell them you will not testify, and that you accused the wrong man. You will also end things with Maxwell. You don't deserve to be with my best friend's son. You will cut all ties to my family and his immediately. You have 48-hours to do so and if this is not done Betty Mae will see an early grave. I had mercy on your family and you have the nerve to rat on that man and cause more trouble. I thought you learned. I've lived a miserable lonely life, not having the love of a mother, and being denied a relationship with the man I love, now it's time for you to see what that feels like. Call the police about this if you want to and by the time I'm done you won't have a family left, that's a promise. With Love, La'Draysha.. I shook my head at the fact that she had the nerve to begin saying she hoped I was doing well and end her threatening letter "with love." I wish that bitch knew love because if she did, she wouldn't be doing the foul shit she does. I wanted to show Maxwell the letter that night but I knew he'd go straight to his mother or even worse, he'd confront La'Draysha. She'd killed people before so I had no doubt that she would make good on the promise to get rid of my family. Therefore, I did what I had to do, ending things with Maxwell by lying to him and everyone else saying that I just needed time to heal.

Chapter 15

DANDRIDGE

"Maturity comes when you stop making excuses and start making changes." –Billie Dureyea Shell

I stood at the door, patiently waiting for Cecelia to answer. It was my weekend to have the kids and so far our arrangement had been working well. We were even getting along. "Hi," she greeted me. Cecilia had answered the door, looking absolutely stunning. "H-Hi," I responded, speechless for only a millisecond. "You look gorgeous." That was an understatement. She was wearing a short red dress with a pair of black pumps. Her hair was pulled up into a neat bun and her soft red lipstick screamed kiss me. "Umm ...where are the kids?" I asked as I looked around. I didn't see my girls anywhere. "Oh, they're with your mother. I thought she called you," I knew she was lying. "You know my mother didn't call me because you know that she no longer has my number," I replied in an irritated tone but I couldn't stop staring at her. She really didn't look like a woman who'd just recently given birth. I almost forgot why I divorced her. "Well, have a seat if you'd like," she said invitingly, pulling me from my thoughts. "I'm not leaving home for another hour." "No, I better go. If the kids aren't here I don't have a reason to be." I turned and began walking toward the door when I heard Cecilia call my name. I turned around to face her, only to see that she'd unzipped the dress and it was now lying on the floor, draped over her ankles. "Dear Lord, help me," I whispered. "I think you should stay a while," she said as she stepped out of the dress and walked closer to me, pressing her succulent breast to my chest. "I miss you Dan," she whispered, standing on her tiptoes to kiss me. I turned my head and her lips found my cheek. "What's wrong? Do you not find me beautiful?" I looked at her in all of her glory and that's when I realized that I truly did love Sharon, and I seriously didn't want to lose her. "It's not that, Cecelia," I explained softly. "It's not that at all. The old me would have you bent over doing the buck by now, but I love Sharon and I can't hurt her like that." I regretted being honest as soon as the words left my lips. "So you could cheat on me and Shanice, but not Sharon?" Fire flashed in her eyes. "We weren't worth you being honest or loyal, but this slut is?" "Don't you ever in your life come out your mouth and call her a slut or any other name, other than Sharon, again," I threatened her. "That woman is the best thing that ever happened to me, and I won't let you, or anybody else, disrespect her!" Cecelia's mouth dropped at the sound of my words and the thunder they seemed to bring. "Dan, I –" "Put your damn clothes on," I interrupted her as I exited the apartment. I couldn't help but smile as I walked to my car. Sharon had really changed me, and I was really starting to like this new guy.

*****

"You didn't fuck her?" Sharon looked at me like it was hard to believe my story. "No, I told her to put her damn clothes back on and that she wouldn't disrespect you. I love you so much, I can't lose you by making the same mistakes I've always made." She smiled like a kid in a candy store. "I believe you ...and I know you're different. I don't think you would have mentioned this thing with Cecilia at all, if you would have cheated on me with her." She placed her hands on my face and brought her lips to mine. "I love you, Dandridge Harris." I pulled her into my arms and looked into her eyes. "Baby, I don't know what you're doing to me but please, keep doing it."

Chapter 16

LA'DRAYSHA

Cecelia sat beside me in tears. We had developed a surefire plan to get her and Dan back together and, according to her, he wouldn't bite. "You were completely naked and he said no?" I was confused. I'd never known my son to turn a woman down. Women were his weakness ...that boy couldn't say no. "He actually told me to put my clothes back on. I was so embarrassed," she cried. "Stop all that crying, girl," I chided her. "You need tougher skin. This isn't over... you'll get him back. I don't want my son affiliated with that family at all, outside of providing for my grandson." "But he loves her and he's not even talking to you," she said, stating the obvious. "If I can keep Shanice and Maxwell apart, surely I can get Sharon to leave my son, if he refuses to leave her." I should have checked my surroundings before I spoke. "Bitch, didn't I tell you not to fuck with my son?" I heard Tina's voice and I knew she'd lost all her cool points with God over all that cursing she'd just done. "Did I say Max," – my words were cut short when I felt Tina's hands wrapped around my throat. I was slowly losing consciousness and Cecelia looked as if she was too shocked to move. "My son was in love with that girl and because of you, they're not together! You don't quit, do you? You better fix this shit or you're down a friend! Your kids have already left your raggedy deceitful ass, it won't be too long before Jamie leaves you hanging, and now you want to mess up our friendship." Tina was pissed but she let me go, standing silently as I struggled for air. "I'll fix it," I rasped, coughing out my words. "Max is too good for her," Cecelia spoke up. Now this heffa finds a voice, I thought. "Maxwell is my son and if he's happy, I'm happy for him. Y'all bitches need prayer," Tina said as she grabbed her purse and headed for the door. Damn. I knew I'd have to find some way to get Maxwell and Shanice to at least talk, but how?

Chapter 17

MAXWELL

"Honesty and loyalty are key. If two people can be honest with each other about everything, that's probably the biggest key 2 success." –Taylor Lautner

"You ready?" I asked Kimberly. She seemed to be taking forever to pack her clothes for the trip to LA. I'd sent my demo to so many record labels, it was ridiculous but I'd finally gotten a call to meet up with Infinity Records, an up and coming label in Los Angeles. "Yes, I'm coming. I'm just trying to pick outfits that don't make me look fat," she pouted. I laughed at her. "Baby, you're barely showing." Kim was two months along and had developed a small pudge, but not enough that anyone might notice that she was pregnant. She hadn't even had to purchase new clothes yet. I wrapped my arms around her waist and kissed the side of her neck. "I'm ready for you to start showing though, so I can show all of my babies off to the world." I was truly happy. Kimberly hadn't been the honest type when we were younger, but I knew she was the one for me the first week after we got together, when she sat me down and told me how we ended up running into each other again.

Four Months ago...

"Maxwell, we need to talk," Kim announced as she came into the kitchen wearing a white lace thong and one of my t-shirts that she'd cut up and made her own. Though I knew we needed to communicate if this was going to work, all I really wanted to do at this moment was feast on her like a predator who'd just caught its prey. I walked over to Kim and pulled her into my arms. "Can we talk later?" I asked as I placed soft kisses on her neck. "No, we have to talk now," she answered me, looking worried. "I don't want anything stopping us from continuing in our relationship." "Relationship?" I asked. Up until now, we hadn't made anything official. "Well, whatever this is we're doing," she said, waving her hand for emphasis. "I'd like this thing we are doing to continue without being based on any lies." "Okay," I answered, bracing myself for the worst since it sounded important. "Well ...what's up?" Her eyes were already watering and I didn't understand why she'd have reason to cry. We'd only been messing around a week. What could be that bad? She took a deep breath and started talking. "We didn't just run into each other that night at Jazz 101. It was set up." I lifted my brow as she talked. This should be real interesting, I thought as I crossed my arms and leaned against the counter. "I ran into Dan's mom one day at the hospital," she continued. "My mom had just died of cancer and Ms. Harris was there for her Chemo. She spotted me in the hallway, crying over my mother, and walked over to see what was wrong. We went down to the hospital café and talked for a while and I don't know... I guess she made me feel comfortable enough to share certain details of my life with her. She asked me if I ever regretted our break-up and I told her yes, I did ...every day. She told me that she could arrange for us to talk but getting back with you would be on me because she was on good knowledge that you'd just gotten out of a relationship." I clinched my jaw tight because, as she talked, things were starting to make a lot of sense but I wanted all of the details before I reacted to her confession. In my silence, I urged Kim to continue. "I told her I'd like that and we exchanged numbers. The next thing I knew she was calling me, telling me to wear something eye catching and get my ass down to Jazz 101 because someone told her they'd seen you in there. I don't know if she was having you followed or if it was a coincidence but I did as she said." I wasn't surprised at all because this wasn't the first time Dan's mom had interfered in my relationship with Shanice. "Is there anything more?" I asked, feeling as if she was leaving something out. She paused for a second before speaking again. "Yes, Max," Kim sighed, her voice breaking a little. "She told me to at least get you into bed, if nothing else, and at least try to trap you by getting pregnant." I cut her off quick. "So what ...you're here to trap me? This shit has happened to me before," I responded angrily, furious this woman was still trying to control my life. "This woman doesn't stop. Look, if you're pregnant, you need to..." I stopped myself because I couldn't bring myself to tell a woman to get rid of my baby. "First of all, if I were pregnant, I wouldn't know," she explained. "We've only been back at it for a week. Second of all, Max, I wouldn't betray you like that. I've done you wrong in the past. I can't do it again. That's why I'm being honest with you now. I'm letting you know that this, us, was not a mistake. We didn't just happen." I sat on the barstool, thinking silently for a moment. I appreciated Kim's honesty. It was unbelievable that even cancer hadn't stopped Miss Harris from trying to ruin Shanice's life. I had no idea what she'd done to make Shanice break up with me but whatever the reason, I was pissed inside. If only Shanice could have done like Kim and come to me, maybe I could have helped her and we would still be together. "Thank you for telling me," I finally said. "I don't want us to lie to each other," Kim said as she looked into my eyes, trying to read my thoughts. "We won't. But what I want you to do is keep talking to Dan's mom and make her believe you're still following through with her plans. That woman is crazy and will do anything to make sure that Shanice and her family members all suffer." "Okay." I kissed her and in that moment, I knew Kim was the woman for me. I'd have to let go of the feelings I'd carried so long for Shanice. Shanice would never stop keeping secrets and secrets always hurt more than they helped.

Present Day...

Kim and I checked in for our flight and found out it

had been delayed due to mechanical issues. We walked around the airport and stopped at the Chili's closest to our gate because Kim was craving a cheeseburger. All I could think about was how Dan's mom brought us back together, not knowing that Kim wasn't the same conniving and dishonest woman as she had been when we were younger. I still longed for Shanice sometimes but I knew I could never love her in the same way again. She'd broken my heart for bullshit reasons not once but twice; it was doubtful she would ever grow up. "You're thinking about her again, aren't you?" Kim said accusingly, snapping me out of my thoughts. "No." I started to lie but then, I decided against it. "Well, yes ...but not in the way you think. I'm thinking about what a blessing it turned out to be that she broke my heart is all." I was being truthful. "Really?" Kim lifted her brow and a glimmer of happiness sparked in her eyes. "Yes, really! Had she not broken my heart, I wouldn't be here with you ...and I wouldn't be as happy as I am now," I replied, taking her small hands in mine. "I love you, Kimberly, with my whole heart." "I love you too, baby," she smiled and I

Chapter 18

SHANICE

I sat on the sofa with Sharon and played with Elijah. It was really awkward being there because I knew Dan was in the other room sleeping, and it was still very hard to wrap my head around the fact that they'd been together for the past five months. "So have you talked to Maxwell?" Sharon was first to break the silence. "No, I've been calling and texting him but he hasn't answered so I decided I'd just let it go," I answered, lowering my eyes to the floor "Seems that he has," I added, feeling so stupid for all the decisions I'd been making. "Well maybe I can be of some help, or Miss Tina," she shrugged. "I'm not calling his mom. I really want to talk to him and explain why we aren't together, but I don't know if I'd be interrupting his life." I had been trying to find out information about what Max was up to but never got anything more than the conformation that he was out of the Army. And I only got that because I think his friend Jackson got tired of me calling his work number. "Well, I'm just glad you finally started speaking to me again. I thought this situation had ruined everything." She gave a soft smile. I had spent four months not speaking to her or Tameka. After everything happened, I was unable to deal with either of them. One of my sisters was in love with the first man I ever loved and the other was going off on the pretense that I thought I was better than her. I was so tired of all the drama and trouble that seemed to never end. Elijah fell asleep in my lap and I decided to put him in his crib. I eased him gently into the crib and tucked him in without so much as a whimper. I couldn't help but smile as I thought about what a pleasant baby he was, and hope that someday my future child would be as sweet. "You hungry? I can go get food," I offered after tucking him in. "No, Dan is supposed to cook when he wakes up." She looked away from me when she said that and I knew why. Dan had surely told her that he had rarely lifted a finger while he was with me. "Wow," I said softly. "Okay. Well, turn the TV on or something …it's too quiet in here." She picked up the remote and I regretted my suggestion as soon as BET came up on the screen. 'You are about to see the world premiere from this hot new artist Max Taylor the song is called I'll Remember!' the VJ yelled into the mic as Max stood beside him, smiling from ear to ear. He looked so good and the audience seemed to love him, clapping and cheering enthusiastically to hear his song. I watched as Maxwell's video played and the lyrics brought tears to my eyes because I felt like he was calling me out. "I'll remember how you left me, With a bottle full of lies, I'll remember how he hurt you, And you came running to my house, I'll remember that I loved you, Like I'll never love again, I'll remember how I made you, More than just my friend, But you, You don't care about, No one but yourself You don't care about, the way I felt when you left, You don't care about, the way my heartaches for you You don't care about, the fact that we're through." Tears streamed down my face as Sharon stared at me, not really knowing what to say. "Fuck you, Max," I said through my tears. I couldn't believe he was calling me selfish and saying I didn't care about him. I left because I cared about him. I couldn't believe this was my life right now. As the video finished, I heard the VJ's voice as the crowd went wild. 'Oh man! That video was hot! So tell me where did you get the inspiration for this song? You wrote it yourself, right?' "Yeah man, I did," Max replied, smiling as he spoke. "I wrote it about five months ago, before I even had a deal. I was in a place where someone I loved really hurt me and I just needed to get it out." 'So ... you still love her?' the VJ asked and you could hear a pin drop in Sharon's house and on the TV as Max took his time in answering. "Nah, man, she's just a past mistake," he said as he shook his head. I broke down even more. A past mistake... is that really how he feels, I thought. "I'm glad I didn't have your baby, you fucking bastard," I said without thinking. I'd forgotten Sharon was there, I was so caught up in my emotions. 'Alright, man. I wish you much success because right now, people are loving you ...and loving this new single!' "Thank you, man. I really appreciate it and I appreciate all the love I've been getting," Max beamed. "It's a dream come true." They dapped each other up. 'Okay, y'all know what to do! To vote for I'll Remember on the count down, just go online to--.' Sharon turned the TV off as the VJ was giving the details to the crowd and everyone at home on how to vote for Maxwell's video. I could tell Sharon wanted to say something, as she'd been watching me like a hawk, but she let me cry for a moment. I couldn't believe Max was out there, talking about me like I was nothing to him. If I didn't know what he was doing before, I definitely knew now. "You okay?" Sharon finally asked. "I will be," I answered sadly. I wanted to kick, scream, and throw something. "You said you're glad you didn't have his baby," Sharon lifted her brow. "What baby?" "I found out I was pregnant a month after Max and I broke up. He wasn't talking to me or answering my text messages, so I had an abortion to save us both the trouble," I admitted. "But Shannie, you wanted kids so bad, and Max would have been the perfect daddy," she said, shocked that I had terminated the baby. I almost wanted to slap her. "Look, I know Dan may have told you my life story, but stay out of it. Max wouldn't have been perfect for shit! You see what he's doing now? Acting like I was the worst thing that ever happened to him, so do me a favor and leave it alone," I said raising my voice as I grabbed my things and headed for the door. Sharon was my sister and I was damn sure Dan had filled her in on a lot of my life, but we weren't that close yet, not close enough for her to think she knew what was best for me and my life. I needed Meka and I needed her now.

Chapter 19

LA'DRAYSHA

I sat at the table across from Danae, neither of us saying a word. In our silence, I couldn't help but notice that she looked absolutely gorgeous, as always. Danae was the spitting image of me when I was her age, mocha brown with slanted hazel eyes and beautiful full lips. My daughter had the physical shape that most women longed for. She was average height, standing at five foot six and wore heels like nobody's business. People always thought we didn't get along because we were so much alike. In many ways, the assumption was true. "So what do you want?" she asked and I immediately sensed a hint of attitude. "I want you to tell everybody the truth so your sister Carla can stop hating me. And Dan? Well, Dan is mine to work on," I responded.

"His hate for me has nothing to do with you." I was tired of my middle child's hatred toward me, which stemmed from all of the lies that Danae and I had told. Everyone had thought I was the evil one, but it wasn't always me. When Tina told me to fix the situation with Maxwell and Shanice, I had decided that I was going to right a lot of my wrongs. "And what truth would that be?" she asked, testing me. "Tell them that it wasn't me who cut the breaks on your little boyfriend's car all those years ago." "Nobody said you did," she smirked. "And that's not the reason Carla doesn't like you. Carla doesn't like you because she knows what happened before that." I couldn't believe Danae had told Carla the secret we'd agreed not to tell anyone.

Twelve years ago...

"Danae!" I yelled Danae's name as she ran past me to her bedroom. Her clothes were ripped and I could hear her crying. I was praying that she'd only been in a fight. Danae had always had trouble with the other girls at school. I felt it was because they were jealous of how pretty she was, compared to the rest of them. Not to mention, she was dating the finest, most athletic guy in school, Camden Moser. Danae and Camden had been together since the sixth grade and the other girls still couldn't stand it now that they were seniors and planning to get married after high school, but I hated him and wanted him to leave my daughter alone. There was something about that boy which had always seemed off. I had tried to threaten him a few times and he still wouldn't leave my daughter alone. I walked into Danae's bedroom and stood there quietly for a moment as she cried into her pillow. I finally walked over and sat beside her on the bed, gently placing my hand on her back. "What's wrong, baby?" I asked her in my most soothing voice. "I need my daddy," she sobbed. "Need him for what?" "To hurt someone," she said as she looked up at me with a cold stare. "Who do you want to hurt and why?" She looked away from me and responded, "I can't tell you." Danae and I always had a very close relationship so I didn't quite understand why she wouldn't tell me what was going on with her, and why she looked as if she'd been in the fight of her life. "You know you can tell me anything, Danae," I comforted her. "What happened to you and why do you want someone hurt?" Tears seemed to fall down her cheeks uncontrollably as she told me what happened. "I went to Camden's house after the game tonight. We were sitting on the couch watching TV, like we always do, and he asked if I wanted to have sex. I told him no because we have always agreed to wait until we get married. He got mad and told me he didn't want to wait anymore because he was the only one of his friends who hadn't had sex yet. I told him I didn't care about that and still wanted to wait. His dad came from around the corner and he looked at me really weird, so I told Camden I wanted to leave. His dad told me I wasn't going anywhere and that if his son wanted to have sex with me I was either going to give to him or he was going to take it. I stood up and walked toward the door and told him I really wanted to go. His dad came to the door and pulled me back in and told Camden to take what he wanted. So he did, I tried my best to fight him ma, I really did." She continued to cry and my blood began to boil as I thought about my own life and how I never wanted this to happen to my children. "You stop that crying," I heard myself say. "Nobody cares about those weak ass tears." Danae looked stunned at what I was saying to her. "Here is what you will do," I continued. I gave her a plan and told her exactly how to follow through on it. "I can't do that," she whispered. "I will go to jail." I could see the fear in her eyes. "You won't go to jail. The police will think it was a mistake, but make sure you do it on a day that he and his father will be together.

It will make you feel better." "No, I would really like to go to the police and tell them I was raped." "Stop being a scared little bitch. You will do as I said because no one cares about what they did. He's a star around here he will get a slap on the wrist," I told her. Her eyes got big and she shook her head in agreement to my plan. A week later, we were watching the news and a report came up about Camden Moser and his father Anthony Moser being killed in a car accident. The report said the brakes malfunctioned and Anthony was unable to stop as he went through a red light at an intersection. He'd been hit by an 18-wheeler and both he and his son had been killed. Danae stood at the doorway of the living room, glaring at me. From that day forward, Danae and I were never the same. She blamed me for turning her into a murderer and because I never mentioned the rape again, she thought I didn't care. I didn't know what else she wanted from me. We'd gotten our revenge and should have been able to move forward with our lives. Present Day... "Why would you tell her what happened before?" I asked emphatically. "Why is that even important?" I was so pissed. "I told her because I was having a hard time dealing with it. You never got me any help," she accused. Her eyes began to water but she took a deep breath and willed herself not to cry. "Hell," she continued, "you should have gotten yourself some help! And I now struggle with trusting people. Every time I feel like someone has wronged me, I have the urge to get even ...in the worst way possible. And the best way to get away from all those feelings has always been to see you as little as possible." I looked at her and crossed my arms. "You're too damn sensitive. You got raped... so the fuck what! You also got revenge, just like I did,--" I stopped myself from talking, as I had never told my children about my life and I didn't want to give out too much information now. "Danae, I need you to get this family to a place where we can at least love each other while I'm still here," I pleaded. "I can get us to a place of love," she smiled. "Thank you. I know your sister and brother will listen to you." I found it odd how easily she had been convinced to let bygones be bygones but I wanted this so badly, perhaps she had enough love for me to put aside our differences and make that happen. "Oh, it's going to be my absolute pleasure." I didn't like the look she had plastered across her face. I hoped my request wouldn't backfire on me, but Danae had always been a selfish child. She had never done anything for someone else's pleasure. Still, a dying woman needs something to hold on to, something to hope for ...and just maybe this cancer will make us better.

Chapter 20

DANDRIDGE

I couldn't believe my ears as I listened in on the conversation Sharon and Shanice were having in the next room. If Shanice had gotten pregnant by Max, it would kill that boy to know that she murdered his baby. Maxwell was nothing like me; he loved Shanice enough to actually want kids with her. I stood there, silently shaking my head in disbelief because I couldn't believe Shanice had done that. She had begged me for a baby and when she finally had it in her hands, she just gave it up. I walked into the living room and kissed Sharon. I knew I'd have to ease into the topic because she'd be mad to know I was listening to their conversation, even though Shanice was rather loud at times. I was also surprised her talking hadn't disturbed Elijah's nap, but he was resting peacefully in the crib. "Hey sexy chocolate," Sharon said as our lips disconnected. "How was your nap?" She'd asked just the question I needed to get the conversation headed in the direction I wanted it to take. "It was good until you and Shannie woke me up in here, talking all loud." "Oh, I'm sorry babe." She made a face. "It's cool, but um... did I hear Shanice say she aborted Max's baby?" I asked. "Leave it alone, Dan." I nodded in agreement that she was right, that it was best for us to leave it alone and stay out of it but Sharon had no idea how much my mother and I were alike. I'd never be able to disregard that kind of information, although I was smart enough to realize that I should have just been happy that Sharon and I were making a life together. Still, I was pissed off at Max's big display in the hospital. Max thought he was going to whoop my ass and steal my woman, and get away with it without having to pay the price. The way my family was set up, we didn't take too kindly to people intentionally trying to hurt us. Well, at least La'Draysha Harris didn't. "So what are we going to do tonight?" Sharon asked, snapping me out of my thoughts. "We are going to lay out on this big ass couch, cuddle up and watch Netflix." "We always do that," she whined. "Well, you're not giving up the goods so I'm fresh out of ideas." I was beginning to get really frustrated with the fact that I'd been with Sharon five months and she still wasn't having sex with me. I had said she was worth the wait but that was only a gesture I'd hoped would make her feel good enough to give up the draws. "There is so much more we can do," she smiled, ignoring my attempt to put sex on the bargaining table again. "I'm going to see if Meka can babysit and if she can't, I'll call my dad so we can go out." "Go out where?" I really wasn't feeling the urge to go out. My urges could be handled right here on the couch but if that's what Sharon wanted, I suppose I was down. "I don't know. Why don't you start thinking about it?" She kissed me on the cheek and disappeared into the bedroom to make her calls for a sitter and get ready. I had no idea where to take her but I knew I better start trying to figure it out.

*****

"Funny seeing you here," my mother said as she opened the door. "Your father isn't here." I looked at her like she'd lost her damn mind. "My father hasn't been here for years." She laughed, "I thought maybe you came to talk to Jamie, because you sure act like you don't know me anymore."

"Oh my God, mom, can you let that go?" I was already agitated with her and I hadn't even fully walked through the threshold. "I really just came over here so you could pass a message to your best friend, Tina. Shanice was pregnant by Max and had an abortion." I knew the grin on my face gave away my intentions; that was confirmed with her response. "Hmm so he is my son after all," my mom speculated with the voice of an evil Queen from a fairytale. She acted as if she was talking more to herself than to me. "What do you mean by that?" "Oh, nothing son," she replied pleasantly. "Thanks for the information. I'll be sure to let her know. How is my grandson, by the way?" "He's good, getting big," I smiled. As uncomfortable as it was to be standing there, speaking to my mother, I couldn't help but smile warmly while talking about Elijah. "I'm sure," my mom said coldly. She was acting very strange and I was beginning to feel even more awkward as I talked with her. "Okay, well I'm going to leave." I turned to walk toward the door. "I'm not doing your dirty work for you, Dandridge," I heard her say. "Excuse me?" I turned back toward her. In her right mind, my mother would never turn down the opportunity to bring trouble and pain down on that family

"You're a part of Shanice's family now. You're in love with

her sister. I'm not going to do anything about this situation, unless you play by my rules." I knew there was going to be some type of catch. It always was with my mother. She was becoming even more calculating with her illness, which I found annoying as hell but also impressive. "What are your rules and I'll let you know," I replied, crossing my arms as I glared at her. "It's simple. Take Cecelia back. She's a real sweet girl...," she began but I threw up my hands, cutting my mother off. "Look, if you love Cecelia so much, why don't you date her? I'm with who I want to be with and nothing is going to stop me from being with Sharon, especially not you. You're done toying with my life." "Oh but because you're upset with Max and Shanice, you'll let me toy with theirs?" She began to laugh. "As much as you and your sisters hate me, you and Danae are cut from the same damn cloth. You're just like me." I looked at her with interest. Why did she bring Danae's name into it? "Danae hates you and hasn't spent any real time with you since she graduated high school. How can you even pretend to know what she's like?" "She's my child, I know," she answered, straightening her posture as if to shake off the accusations I had thrown in her direction. "And before you start changing your life for Sharon, ask her about what she was doing before I met her and got her that job at the Real Estate firm. You keep running from Cecelia but I promise you, baby boy, she's the best thing for you. Now leave my house," she turned away from me and headed up the steps. I was curious to know what I would find out when I did talk to Sharon.

Chapter 21

MAXWELL

"**B**aby, that was awesome!" Kim screamed as I walked back into my dressing room. She was practically jumping up and down in excitement. "Yeah, it was cool." I tried to downplay tonight's success, turning my back to her as I took off my jacket and placed it on the nearby clothing rack. It was funny how, when you saw celebrities and the clothes they wore, you would assume they were all theirs what I'd learned quickly was that most of the clothes were only borrowed to help promote the brand. "So did you mean it?" I heard her ask softly. "Mean what?" I mumbled, straightening my shirt as I turned around. I knew what she was asking but for some reason, I wanted her to say the words. "That she was just a mistake?" I walked over to where she stood, waiting for me to reassure her. Her beautiful brown skin seemed to glow more and more each day. Kim was not the woman I thought I would end up with, or even the woman I thought I'd love as much as I did, and if I had to spend every day proving to her that I no longer wanted Shanice then that's what I would do. "Of course I meant it, baby." I leaned down to press my lips against her soft full lips. "She was the mistake that lead to the best decision I ever made." I looked into her eyes and they started to get glossy. Ever since we found out she was pregnant, her emotions had been all over the place. "Why are you crying?" "I just hope you never stop loving me," she sniffled. "I won't," I promised as I wiped her tears away with my hand and held her close to me for what seemed like forever.

*****

Kim and I walked into the house a little after midnight. We'd had a ball in New York and it felt good being in a relationship that didn't have a whole bunch of secrets. Dan's mom was dead wrong for trying to use these women to trap me, but I was glad she'd brought Kim back into my life. "Baby, it's like a ton of mail here," I heard Kim yell to me. I walked into the kitchen and looked at the mountain of mail she'd just placed on the counter. "It can all wait." I pulled at her hand, leading her to the living room. "What if it's important?" "Nothing is more important than me making love to you... right here, right now," I answered, giving her the sexiest look I knew how to give. I had been so tired in New York, going from TV interview to radio interview and then dinner meetings to promote myself and my brand. I was trying to bring back real music, something that truly expressed how a person was feeling and so far, the world had really embraced me. "Oh really? I didn't know if you remembered what that was anymore," she said playfully. "I'll show you what I remember." I pulled her down on my lap and smiled because she could feel my already erect manhood. "You want me that bad?" "Worse," I admitted as I began kissing her while using my hands to unbutton the blouse she wore. I freed her breasts and took them into my mouth, one by one, teasing her nipples until they became hardened with desire. She threw her head back, enjoying my every touch and kiss. "I love you," I whispered. She stood in front of me as she slipped the blouse completely off and tossed it on the nearby chair before dropping to her knees. "I love you too," she smiled as she unfastened my pants. I stood for a second so I could step out of them and take off my boxers, allowing her better access to me. I sat back on the couch and she looked into my eyes before taking me into her warm mouth. I laid my head back on the couch and enjoyed the back and forth motion of her taking in as much of me as she could. Her technique had me feeling like I was in another world. She brought her lips down to my head and began to suck on it slowly and then increased her speed as she rubbed my shaft with her hand. "Damn Kim!" I heard myself say. She looked up at me and as soon as our eyes connected, I was a goner. I released myself in her mouth as she continued to rub my shaft, knowing that would get me aroused again. She stood again, dropping her pants and I hardened with anticipation. She sat on down on it and began to ride me like a stallion as I met her rhythm with my every thrust. Ever since she'd gotten pregnant, our positions were limited but I was happy she could still ride. I loved making her feel like she was in control. She moved slowly, making love to me like she always did. We had our rough moments but this was not one of them, and her movements were driving me crazy. I held her hips and moved under her to make sure she could feel every inch of me. "Ah Max," she whispered my name.

"Say it again." "Max," she said a little louder. She began to grind a little harder on me and that's when I knew she was nearing her climax. "Babe," she said. "Yes?" "Babe..." she began to tremble and I knew she'd gotten hers. I pumped myself in her a little bit faster and she stopped me as she slowly lifted herself until only the head of my penis was inside of her. She tightened herself around me and began to tease me. She knew exactly what she was doing as I exploded. "Sensitive spot," she grinned. "Oh, this isn't over," I told her as I pulled her into me and held her.

Chapter 22

LA'DRAYSHA

I sat outside of Betty Mae's house, not really knowing why I was there. I kept telling myself I was done with this family but as I sat at home thinking about the fact that I was dying, it started to piss me off knowing that my bitterness started with Betty Mae. Why should I die and she still be alive? And every time I thought about how she acted as if she didn't know that she'd ruined my life, it made me that much more resentful. I watched the liquid substance glide back and forth across the sides of the glass as I tipped the small bottle to and fro a couple of times, holding it up to the light. "This is your last hoorah with this family," I told myself. I knew Dan wanted me to go further with the Shanice and Maxwell situation, but I couldn't meddle in that any more than I already had. My friendship with Tina was on the line and I only knew one way to get Maxwell to talk to that girl. I had promised Kimberly I'd keep Max and Shanice away from each other but I felt like I'd done a good deed and given her what she desired most, Maxwell's love. If that love was real, it would be able to stand, even when Shanice and Max accidently ran into each other. I stayed in the car for a while, waiting patiently for Melissa to finally leave the house. I had taken a gamble because I didn't know if she would be going anywhere that day, but I needed her gone to execute my plan and go undetected. "You ready?" I looked over and, in my passenger seat, saw my mother staring back at me. I'd forgotten to take my medication and here she was. "Never been more ready for anything," my mother said dryly. "You know once you do this, you cannot take it back." "I don't want to," I responded with similar emotion. "Okay, so what are you waiting on? Melissa is gone and you're still sitting here, you're giving her way too much time to come back." My mom was right. I was stalling for no reason, as Melissa had walked out of the house a good five minutes ago. I reached for the handle on the car door but was stopped before I could pull it toward me. I watched as a woman walked through the yard and stopped in front of Betty Mae's front door. "What is she doing here?" I whispered.

Chapter 23

SHANICE

"I'm so happy we're doing this! I needed something to take my mind of off Maxwell," I said as I took a sip of my Abreu Vineyard Cappella Proprietary Red wine. Reagan had blown off his girlfriend to take me to the Napa Valley California because he knew I had a secret passion for wine. He had arranged for an evening of wine and painting and it was awesome, even if he did choose a female nude as our subject. "I'm glad something is taking your mind off of the drama back in North Carolina. Have you thought about what you're going to do with yourself?" Reagan asked, keenly aware of my lack of plans for the future. I grew quite for a minute as I thought, savoring my wine as I wondered how he would receive the truth. I figured I should tell him what was on my agenda. He wasn't as judgmental as Tameka or as emotional as Sharon, so I had no doubt that he was definitely the best person to talk to. "Well, when I get back, I'm going to pay Max a visit. I don't care about Kim. He's ended relationships before because he loved me and if he still does, he'll let go of his rebound and we'll be able to move forward and get married. I'm going to tell him everything and just pray that he forgives me." Reagan looked at me like I'd just lost the last little bit of sense God had granted me. "And when that doesn't work?" "What do you mean when?" I was surprised by Reagan's pessimism. "It might work... I have the truth on my side." "He called you a mistake on national television, Shanice. That man is over you," he whispered before looking at the model and continuing in his efforts to paint her. "If it doesn't work ...and that's a very big if, I'm going to pack my things and move. I don't know where I will go. I really don't care, anywhere that will get me far away from all of the bullshit. I'm tired of Miss Harris constantly controlling and manipulating my life, and going after everyone in my family. I just want to get away from it all, but not without trying to repair my relationship with Max." "Good luck," he shrugged, "but anyway, back to our

Max free weekend. That was the first and last discussion about him, agreed?" "I agree," I responded, lifting my glass to my lips before continuing to paint the beautiful female model who sat frozen in her position in front of us.

*****

If you want to see Maxwell he is at Cape Fear Botanical Garden, read the text message from a number I didn't recognize. Who is this, I replied. Miss Harris. Now I was really confused. Why would Dan's mom be trying to help me now? She was the one who'd ruined us but now, all of a sudden, she was concerned with helping me talk to him? Something wasn't right about that. Do you think I'm dumb enough to fall for your setup? I typed my response angrily, wishing this woman could feel the pain she caused me every day. Do I think you're dumb? The answer is yes. Do I know that he's been avoiding your every attempt to talk to him? The answer is also yes. I gave you a location. Do what you will with it. Good-bye. I didn't know if I should run to my car and head straight to the Botanical Garden or if I should just ignore her text and keep trying to contact him on my own. Miss Harris had no reason to help me and I didn't believe that she'd suddenly had a change of heart after years of tormenting me, but I knew this also might be my only shot at fixing things with Maxwell. I just prayed he was there like she said, and that he would be alone. He'd expressed to me many times that the garden was his thinking place, a place where many of his song lyrics would come to him, and a special place he'd never shared with anyone. It had been six months since we had ended things and I didn't know if Maxwell had changed now that he had Kim back in his life.

Chapter 24

DANDRIDGE

I walked into Sharon's apartment, making sure to slam the door behind me. "What is your problem?" she asked, looking over at me. I noticed she didn't have the baby in her arms like she normally did when I came home. We had agreed not to hold him all of the time but when I'd leave, Sharon would sit and hold that boy for hours on end. "Where's Elijah?" "He's with my dad," she replied. "What's wrong with you?" I glared at her for a moment before I told her what was wrong. "Where exactly did my mom find you?" She lowered her eyes for a moment and looked at me like it pained her to say. "At the real estate agency, I was…" I put my hand up to stop her from repeating the same lie that she and my mother had clearly been telling everyone. "You have been encouraging me to be honest with you and everyone else in my life so Sharon, please don't lie to me," I said bluntly. "Whatever the truth is, I can handle it." She took a deep breath before starting to speak again. "I was a stripper ...at VIP's." As soon as the name of the club rolled off her lips, I shook my head to make sure I wasn't hearing things. "So you like women?" I asked, although I was fairly certain that I already knew the answer and didn't want to believe it. How did my mom and I both end up sharing our beds with someone from the gay community? "Yes and no," she sighed, which only confused me more. "How can your answer be both yes and no?" I responded with impatience in my voice. I'd tried so hard to be honest with this girl and now, it was like I didn't know her at all. "Either you like women ...or you don't." "I do," Sharon replied quietly, "but I'm not gay. I just like to switch things up from time to time. I've only had two serious relationships with females. Both wanted me to stop being with men and I couldn't, so I decided to date girls whenever the mood struck and exclusively date only men." I shook my head as she sat there, explaining herself as if there was nothing wrong with her choices. "So my mother got you the real estate job?" I sat down on the edge of the sofa, trying to process all of this new information. "Yes. When I first met Miss Harris, I explained to her how I didn't want to strip anymore. I told her that I had a realtor's license and a degree that I wanted to put to use. Two days later, I had a job." I slouched back on the couch. "Wow," I said as I rubbed my face with my hands. "Were you ever going to tell me about your bi-curious lifestyle?" She looked away before she answered, "I was ...but I was waiting on you and Cecelia to get in a real good place first." "What does Cecelia have to do with anything?" She smiled a little as she responded, "Well, I know you've had all kinds of experiences with women so it would be nothing new to you. Cecelia is bad. I would have been mad if you would have cheated on me with her, but I'm okay with inviting her..." "Wait, wait, wait!" I interrupted her, immediately pissed by her admission. My blood was boiling. I looked at Sharon as if I was seeing her for the very first time. "You've been making me wait to have sex like it was going to be something special, and really mean something to the both of us, but this entire time you've been wanting to have a threesome with me and my ex? You are real fucked up." "Dan..." She began to speak, to plead her case, but decided against it when she saw the expression on my face. She was a stranger to me.

Everything I thought I knew about the girl I had been living with was a lie, and in the process, I couldn't help but feel that she had forced me to live her lies and become a fake too. And if she was so liberal minded and experimental about sex before, why had she waited until she got with me to become some kind of born again virgin? "I need some air," I mumbled angrily as I stood to walk toward the door. I didn't know if this was going to be the end for Sharon and myself, but I definitely needed to think about the future, and if this was the kind of relationship I wanted and could be happy with, or the type of home life I would want for my son. I walked outside and remembered that my mom said she wasn't going to do my dirty work for me with Max. I was so caught up in what she'd said about Sharon that I'd forgotten to send a text to his phone. My world wouldn't be the only one that was full of confusion tonight.

Chapter 25

MAXWELL

"**B**ae, come on!" I yelled to Kimberly. She was getting dressed very slowly as always and I needed her to be on time for the special plans I had made. She'd been my backbone through this whole music deal and a great support as I was transitioning out of the Army. I wanted to take her out and show her how much I appreciated her efforts and understanding. When she hadn't answered, I sat my phone on the counter and went into the room to see what the holdup was. My mouth dropped to the floor as soon as I walked into the bedroom and Kim turned around. Her golden skin shined in the soft light of our room, and the teal colored dress she was wearing complimented her complexion so well. "I'm ready, dang!"

She smiled her infectious smile as I shook my head, smiling back at her. In this moment, I felt so extremely lucky. "Thank you, God, for giving me this beautiful woman," I said aloud. "He says you're welcome," she giggled, winking as she passed by me, headed toward the kitchen. "I just have to grab a sparkling water." I was right on her heels. "You have a text," she called back to me. I could see my phone lighting up on the counter. I picked it up and saw Dan's name flash across the screen. "It's from Dan and he's the last person I have time for tonight," I told her, setting the phone back down. "Let me see what he has to say," she volunteered. "If it's going to ruin your mood, I won't say a word." Before I could object, she picked up the phone and slid her finger across the screen to unlock it. I saw her face go from happy to horrified as she put her free hand over her mouth. "What's wrong?" I asked, grabbing the phone from her. There was no way to prepare for the text message that Dandridge sent. I know we ain't cool but I'm sorry things went so bad between you Shannie that you made her have an abortion. I guess we're a lot alike. I didn't want a kid with her either. My jaw was clenched together so tight, I thought my teeth might break. "You asked her to have an abortion?" I didn't like the way she was looking at me now.

"Kim, I can't believe that you would even ask me that. I would never tell a woman, no matter what the situation was, to abort my child. If Dan is even telling the truth about this abortion, I promise you that I knew nothing about it. Shanice never said anything about being pregnant." My heart dropped to my stomach as I suddenly remembered the night I asked Shanice to have my baby. I wanted to cry but I didn't need Kim to know the news and the memory had affected me to that extent. "Let's go." I took her hand and left my phone sitting on the counter. Kim and I had a date night to get to and I wasn't going to let Dan and his news ruin it.

*****

"Oh my God, baby!" Kim put her hands to her mouth as she looked at the romantic scene laid out in front of her. I'd rented the Gazebo at the Cape Fear Botanical Garden and had it decorated with a candlelight dinner setting. I hired Grant St. Paul, a world renowned personal chef, to cook the evening meal and had my keyboard set up as well. "I just wanted to show you a little love tonight." I smiled and kissed her cheek before walking around the table and pulling out her chair. When she was seated, I proceeded to my keyboard. "Can I play something special for you?" "Only if it's original," she beamed. "I was hoping you'd say that." I focused my attention on the keys and began to play the song I'd just written for her earlier that evening. 'Baby I know we have a past, But I pray our love will last, Forever, Forever, So today I have to ask, If you will take my hand, In marriage, In marriage, I wanna see you walk down that aisle, And pledge to me your love, Until death do we part, I give my heart, I give my heart' I looked up to see Kim smiling and crying as St. Paul stood beside her, holding a serving tray that displayed the three carat square pink princess cut diamond I'd picked out for her when I returned Shanice's ring. I couldn't believe I was proposing again but I knew this time was right. I was confident that Kimberly wouldn't lie to me the way Shanice had. I stopped playing and got down on one knee in front her. "Kim baby, I love you. You are not only my woman but you are my best friend and the mother of my children." I placed my hand on her stomach. "Will you please make me the happiest and most blessed man in this world and say you'll be my wife?" "Maxwell, don't do this... I love you!" I turned toward the familiar voice that had just interrupted my proposal before Kim could answer. "Shanice?"

Chapter 26

LA'DRAYSHA

I watched as the girl walked out of Betty Mae's house, noticing that she seemed to be in a big hurry. When she was out of sight, I got out of my car and continued my mission. I knocked on the door and waited for a second. Although the door was open, I didn't want to walk in unannounced because I had no idea what had just happened in there. I checked my surroundings and then slowly opened the door. "Betty?" I called out as I walked through the door. No one answered. "Betty?" I called her name again. "I did it for you." Danae's voice startled me. "Why were you here?" "I know what she did to you," she answered. I couldn't believe that she actually had the nerve to smile. "She didn't do anything to me." I found myself defending

Betty Mae, although I had no idea why I would feel compelled to do so. "She did the same thing to you that you did to me in the past. She was the reason you're so fucked up, and you're the reason why history has repeated itself with me. You wanted me to fix the family so that's what I'm doing, and I'm starting with you," she responded, her smile instantly making me feel uneasy, as I was never one to like surprises. "Now that she's gone, maybe you can live the rest of your life... you know, what little life you have left, being a better person." I looked at Danae as if I was seeing a stranger. "Gone? And I thought you hated me," I asked, confused, wondering if something was amiss. My kids all seemed so ready for me to die and yet Danae suddenly would do something so crazy to make my life better. She looked at me and shook her head. "Let's go before Melissa gets back." "Wait. How did you even know I was here?" "I followed you." She stood to the side so I could exit first and neither of us said a word on our way out of the door.

*****

"Thank you!" Tina seemed happy and I already knew why. "Are they back together?" I was praying Maxwell wasn't having it. "I just know they've talked," she smiled

141

with an expression I knew all too well. Tina didn't trust me with the information. "Well, that's good and you're welcome. You know I couldn't lose my best friend so close to the end," I said softly, lowered my head while thinking about the fact that it was very close to the end. I had been feeling myself becoming weaker and weaker as time went by, and there was nothing I could do about it. "Where is Jamie?" she asked, looking around. "I don't know, child," I said, blending the truth with a lie. "I sometimes wonder why we got married ...since he's never here." I didn't want to tell her what was really going on, that Jamie said he needed some time away from me because I was still seeing and talking to my mother whenever I didn't feel up to taking my medication. "Well, your brother knows better. I wish he would call himself trying to stay away from me especially during a time like this." She made a face that told me she had successfully placed Rowland under lock and key. "Well, has Maxwell and Kim found out what their having?" I asked in an effort to change the subject. "No, we just know its twins!" she squealed, gleaming with excitement. Her face was illuminated with happiness and while part of me struggled to bite my tongue, my malevolent side wouldn't let her have this moment of joy. "Well, you know you're actually supposed to have three grandchildren on the way?" I decided to see how much she really knew. "Excuse me?" "Dan came over here the other day talking about how Shanice had an abortion, girl. He wanted me to tell Max, but I told him I wouldn't." She gave me a sideways stare and I waited patiently for her response as she sipped her tea. "Them boys need to get it together! I can't believe Shanice has caused all this madness between those two." "Oh? So now you see why I don't like her?" "No, no. Now I'm not judging the girl and I know that, no matter what, a part of my son is always going to love that girl, but I do feel she could have gone about things a lot differently." I hated when Tina did that. She would let on like she understood and even sympathized with me, and then suddenly backtrack. "I just wish you would find Jesus, Draysha. You would be overcome with such a peace, and your heart would be full of forgiveness." She shook her head. "Listen to this song by Tasha Cobbs," she requested as she reached for her phone and started searching through it for the song. 'You provide the fire, I'll provide the sacrifice, You provide the spirit, And I will open up inside, Fill me up God, Fill me up God, Fill me up God, Fill me up' And as the music played, I really did begin to feel it. I didn't know if it was the words or the voice of the woman who was singing, but there was something that filled the air around us in that moment. I wondered if I should have been listening to Tina over the years when she would encourage me to get saved. The song continued to play and I realized I had tears flowing heavily from my eyes. "I'm sorry," I whispered aloud, talking to God. "I'm so sorry, God," I said again. "What's wrong?" Tina asked. I could hear the hopefulness in her voice. "You're right but it's too late, Tina! I've done way too many bad things," I sighed as I shook my head, trying to blink the tears away. "It's okay. The Lord will still forgive you, girl. He's nothing like us," she said softly with compassion in her voice, making me feel bad for trying to upset her before. It was very cruel of me. "He doesn't hold a grudge, nor is he caught up in bitterness." "So I can get saved right now and the Lord would be okay with me?" That was very hard to believe. "Yes, La'Draysha, you can." "I want to," I heard myself say. Tina took my hands into hers and right before she could open her mouth to pray, there was a knock. "Give me a second," I released her hands and stood to answer the door. "Bitch, you tried to kill my mama!" Melissa had basically tackled me at the door. She was throwing punches like a grown man and in my weakness and shock, I was too helpless to fight back. "Stop, stop," I heard Tina yelling but Melissa wasn't stopping. "I will kill you for the shit you've done to me and my family," I heard Melissa say as she banged my head on the hard wood floor. "I will kill you" – was the last thing I heard before everything faded to black.

Chapter 27

SHANICE

Maxwell had abruptly stopped what he was saying to Kimberly and returned to his feet. I knew that I had forever ruined his romantic proposal to her as he looked in my direction. "Shanice?" "Max, I am so sorry but I love you. Please don't marry her." I was out of line but I had to stop him before he made the commitment to marry someone else. He looked at me and shook his head before looking back at her. "Baby, I'm sorry. I don't even know how she knew we would be here." "I have an idea," Kim sighed, rolling her eyes. "I'm going to look at some of the flowers. Take your time, boo." I watched as she stood and kissed Max on the cheek, clearly unfazed by my presence. That is when tears really began to flow. "She's pregnant?" I asked him, the tone of my voice similar to that of a wounded child. It was a question that he need not respond to, as the answer was in her rounded silhouette and the way she carried herself as she stepped into the garden. Maxwell turned to face me and I watched his expression went from the genuine stare he was giving Kim to being one of anger in an instant. "Shanice, just tell me one thing. Did you kill my baby?" I was stunned, as I had no idea how he could know about that. "Cat got your tongue?" he accused, folding his large arms across his chest. "Max, I…" I began, wanting to tell him the answer to his question. I needed to explain that I only did it because he had ignored me, and that his actions led me to think that he wanted nothing more to do with me. "You, you what?" he interrupted, obviously unwilling to hear my excuses. "You're sorry? You were scared? You what, Shannie?" I just stood there, my eyes full of tears because there was nothing left to say. I could tell that he had already made up his mind about me. It was clear that I would only be part of his past. "I shouldn't have come here," I finally spoke, apologetically. "You're right you shouldn't have," he responded angrily. "Please just leave me and my family be." "Your family?" I was finally growing angry with him and with this entire situation.

"Your family, Maxwell? A few years ago, that woman slept with one of your soldiers while you were deployed. She doesn't love you." He waved me off like I hadn't said a word. "I know this may be hard for you to believe but people really do change and now that we are both older, Kimberly is the best thing that has ever happened to me. She hasn't lied to me yet, although I cannot say the same thing about you. So do me a favor and leave me and my family the hell alone. There is no longer a place for you in my heart or in my life," Max said, raising his voice. He had never spoken to me in such a tone and as I looked into his eyes, I could see the sternness in his glare and could tell he meant every word. "Maxwell, please think about what you're saying." "I've said it." He turned to walk away as I took in the beautiful romantic scene he'd created for his proposal. As he approached her, he returned to one knee and took her hand into his. I couldn't help but think about the night he had proposed to me. It wasn't a bit as romantic as this garden scene but it still meant everything to me. I couldn't stop the tears as I watched him pick her up and embrace her because she'd said yes. I turned to walk away, ready to start making plans to get away from Fayetteville.

*****

I climbed inside my car and tried my best to stop crying as I retrieved my phone from the passenger seat and noticed I had four missed calls from Tameka. I dialed her number, hoping it wasn't too much of an emergency. I knew I couldn't handle anything else right now. "It's about time!" she answered. I could hear the urgency in her voice. "What's going on?" I asked, masking the sad tone in my voice. "Girl, mama is in jail! She tried to kill Miss Harris!" "What? Wait, wait!" Surely I wasn't hearing my sister correctly. "What do you mean 'mama tried to kill her'? What happened?" I definitely wasn't expecting to hear those words. "Something about she wanted to kill grandma but Danae helped grandma out, I don't know. Just meet me and grandma at the jail," Meka said, nearly out of breath as she tried to explain. "We're trying to see if we can get her out." I hung up the phone and sped quickly toward the jail. I had no idea what was going on and I couldn't understand why Miss Harris wouldn't just leave us alone. Hadn't she done enough already? It was because of her that I couldn't have Maxwell, and now she was trying to kill my grandmother. This was a night for the books, I thought.

Chapter 28

DANDRIDGE

"What the hell happened?" I ran right into Jamie, Danae, Carla, Tina, and Rowland as I came bursting through the emergency room doors with Sharon on my heels. Danae turned away looking very guilty and I just hoped she had nothing to do with our mother being hospitalized. "Danae? You know something," I accused, challenging her to tell the truth. "What happened?" "Shanice's mom beat her pretty bad," Tina interjected. "They're trying to stop the bleeding. It's coming from her head so we may be here a while." I was caught completely off guard, as I didn't think Shanice's mom had it in her. "So basically, all her bullshit has come back on her," I reveled. My demeanor changed because I'd taken a couple beatings for my bullshit, and it was about time my mom got hers. "Don't do that, Dan," Tina pleaded as she gave me a motherly glare which served as a warning not to say anything else. There was something about Maxwell's mom that made me feel as if I had to respect her. I was grateful that she and my mom had been friends all of these years because she was the best mother figure I had, thanks to my own mother's unscrupulous antics. "Danae, can I talk to you outside?" I asked my sister, wanting to know what she was hiding. "Yea," she complied, following me through the double doors of the hospital exit as I searched for a private place to talk. When we were safely away from everyone, I turned to look her in the eyes. "Okay, so what's really going on?" I asked, crossing my arms for effect. I wanted the truth. She darted her eyes away from me for a second before she began to share what information she knew. "She was going to kill Betty Mae earlier today. I heard her talking to grandma before I left her house the other day, and she was saying how it wasn't fair that Betty Mae gets to live to a ripe old age while she slowly dies from cancer. She said her whole fucked up life was Betty Mae's fault and if she was going to hell, Betty Mae would be waiting for her at the door." I shook my head in disbelief as

I tried to wrap my head around the crazy things my sister was saying. That's how I knew it was the truth …because anything that crazy had to be tied to our mother. "So I followed her to Betty Mae's and went inside before she had a chance to get out of her car," Danae continued. "I told Betty what was going on and gave her a muscle relaxer …and some sleeping pills that knock you out on spot. So when mama walked into Betty Mae's, she thought I'd done the job for her and I went along with it. I know that sounds crazy but I didn't know what else to do." "So then what…?" I had a pretty good idea about the events that followed but I needed clarity. I needed her to explain everything that had happened up to this point, as things were going to get heated when the news reached everyone. "I guess Betty told Melissa what had taken place and now here we are. I don't know much of anything else and personally, I don't care if the bitch dies," Danae announced as she folded her arms across her chest and pouted like a little kid. "When will all of this stop?" "When your mama dies," Danae spat sharply as she turned to walk back into the hospital. We sat in the emergency room for what seemed like forever. Sharon kept getting up to retrieve coffee and snacks for my family, including herself. I still didn't have much to say to her, and her attempt to be there for me felt odd. All I could think about was how much I wanted things to work but she had put me in a terribly awkward position. I avoided pleasantries with Sharon as I sat there with my eyes closed, pretending not to notice how she was up and down the entire time. "Harris family?" A tall skinny black doctor holding a tablet stepped into the emergency waiting area and called our name. He swiped the screen as if opening documents containing pertinent information about my mother's condition. "Yes?" Jamie responded as if he was a Harris. "Who should I speak with about Miss Harris's condition?" he asked. "Mrs. Foster," Jamie spoke up, correcting the doctor. "I'm her husband, Jamie Foster. You can talk to me." He walked over to an isolated part of the waiting area with the doctor and they began to speak about my mother's condition, referring to the device in the doctor's hands several times. I knew the news wasn't the best when I saw Jamie place his hands over his mouth and noticed the wrinkles which were formed heavily in his brow. After several minutes, they shook hands and Jamie turned to look at all of us before walking back over, slowly. "She can't have any visitors tonight but the doctor said she has some swelling on her brain that could cause amnesia. They don't know how serious her condition is at this time. They're going to wait a couple of days and then run some tests. We will have more answers then, but right now there is a pending issue. The only people she seems to remember is me, Tina, Bobby and Rowland." He looked at all of us like he'd just hurt our feelings. "Cool, so that means I don't have to show my face around here anymore." I got up and headed for the exit. As far as I was concerned, the universe had done me a huge favor today. In reality, it appeared that I had already lost my mother since she didn't remember me. Now it was time for me to figure out my relationship with Sharon.

Chapter 29

MAXWELL

"**S**orry that had to happen to your sister," I said, acting as if I didn't know La'Draysha like that as we talked about what happened to her at the dinner table. I could tell that the event had really effected Rowland because he wasn't as into the conversation as he normally was. "It's okay. I've been praying for a full recovery," he said. "Well, she was about to accept Christ right before it happened," my mom chimed in. "I had just taken her hands into mine and opened my mouth to pray the sinner's prayer with her. I really wish she wouldn't have stopped me to open that door." I looked at my mom as if she'd just fabricated the biggest lie known to man. There was no way La'Draysha Harris was about to accept anybody's God, especially not the one my mother and I served. "Stop looking at me like that. I played that Tasha Cobbs song 'Fill Me Up' for her and she was so touched by it, the tears began to flow. Finally, she was ready to give her life to the Lord," my mom retorted, defending herself. "Oh, that song is powerful," Kim added, agreeing with my mom. "I don't think anything is powerful enough to change that kind of evil. I sometimes think Dan's mom is the devil himself, roaming the earth to destroy everyone and everything in her path. She couldn't touch this family the way she wanted to because we're covered," I added with a smile. "Don't talk about her like that, Max. She's gone through some very real things and no, she didn't know how to deal with it. You've had a relationship with God long enough to know that it is never too late to accept Christ, as long as you still have breath in your body." My mom had grown very serious in the moment. "You're right but with her, I just can't see it," I admitted, shaking my head. I loved Sunday dinners now that my mom and I both had someone by our sides. They didn't seem as lonely as they used to be. It was as if we had finally become a family. "So are the two of you ready? Three more months till the wedding," Kim reminded my mother and her fiancee, changing the subject.

"I'm getting there," Rowland laughed. "Oh hush! You've been trying to do more planning than me," my mom teased, hitting him playfully. Seeing her happy was awesome. However, I couldn't help but be surprised that it was with someone cut from the same cloth as La'Draysha. I didn't understand how her brothers could turn out so good, but she was hell on wheels, wreaking havoc at every turn. "Well, I'm just ready to walk my mom down that aisle and give her to you ...then she can stop getting on my nerves," I joked, dodging her playful swat. "One day you gon' wish I was around to get on your nerves," she said as she missed. I hated when she talked like that, even though I knew she was only kidding. After a few moments, her expression grew serious and she tossed her dinner napkin over her plate. "Well Kim and Rowland, will y'all excuse me and my son? We are going to step outside and talk." She pushed her chair away from the table and I immediately did the same, not knowing what she could possibly want to talk with me about. She certainly had my curiosity as we walked through the French doors of the kitchen and onto the patio. My mom was silent for a minute and I knew it was because she was choosing her words carefully so I waited quietly for her to begin the conversation. "Are you sure you want to marry

Kim, son?" I rolled my eyes, taken aback because this was not what I expected her to say. "Very," I said without looking at her. "I raised you to look a person in their eyes when you're talking to them ...unless you're lying, Maxwell. So I'm going to ask you again," she said with authority but her voice remained soft, concerned. "Are you sure about what you're doing?" "Yes ma, I'm sure." She shook her head. "I normally wouldn't do this but I'm going to tell you something that I think you deserve to know and you can do what you want to with the information. I love Kim and I think the two of you will be awesome parents to those babies, but I cannot keep any more secrets for La'Draysha Harris." I was confused. "What ma? And why are you keeping secrets for that woman?" "I came across a drafted letter to Shanice that was dated about six months ago. La'Draysha has always had a thing about writing letters but she always does a rough draft as if it's school work or something. Son, she threatened to kill Shanice's family if that girl didn't leave you alone. She also told Shanice that she would never be good enough for you and that she had better drop her rape case against that guy." My eyes widened as she spoke and I could tell this secret had been eating at her for some time. "How long ago did you find the letter?"

I asked, steadying myself against the railing as I waited for the answer. "The same day of the incident with Melissa," my mother sighed heavily. "I went over to help her clean up and get things in order, and to thank her for getting you and Shanice to talk. I didn't think you were going to let Shanice go but that was your choice..." I interrupted my mother with another question. "You sent Shanice there?" "Heavens no, but La'Draysha did. I never would have wanted Shanice to be there when you proposed to another woman. You know that's not me." I wanted to be mad but I couldn't muster that kind of emotion against my mother. "La'Draysha told me about the abortion and all I can say is that you need to forgive her. I don't think she did it to hurt you. Shanice probably felt like she was alone ...and in a hopeless situation." My mother's eyes glistened in the evening moonlight, fixed on something in the distance. It felt as if she spoke from experience, perhaps as if she had once faced the same hopelessness and had contemplated a similar decision. "You..." – I started to ask but she cut me off. "I had a daughter when you were only a year old. I gave her up for adoption because your father had left me and I couldn't raise two children alone. I did it because it felt hopeless and I regret it every day," my mother admitted, the tears finally escaping her eyes. I couldn't believe my ears. "Wow. I don't know what to say, mom," I whispered as I pulled my mother into my arms and hugged her tightly. There was no way that I could be upset with her, and I appreciated her honesty. While the conversation between us had brought clarity, it also left me confused and wondering if I was making a mistake.

*****

"So do you want to be with her?" Kim's question hadn't come as a surprise. I sat on the edge of the bed in my Atlanta hotel room with my back to her because I couldn't look at her as I told her what had really taken place between me and Shanice. I had been questioning myself for almost two weeks and the more Kim did to make me love her, the harder it was for me to make a decision. "Maxwell?" She called my name when I didn't answer. I finally turned to face her. "Do... you... want... to be with her?" Her voice had grown a little bit more stern while waiting for me to respond. "I love her, but no Kim I don't want to be with her," I replied honestly, praying she would believe me. "So why would you tell me all of this if you don't want to be with her?" "Like I've told you from day one, I want to keep things honest and truthful between us. You were honest with me about how we got together, so I wanted to be honest with you as well. I've never been a secrets kind of guy," I added. "That gets you caught up and in trouble every time." A slight smile ran across her face. "You're sure?" "Yes baby, I'm sure. I'm yours for life," I said as I flashed a smile which displayed all thirty-two of my teeth. "You better be," she threatened softly as she slid down to the edge of the bed where I had been sitting the entire time to leave a kiss on my bottom lip. "I love you, Maxwell," she said with her lips still slightly touching mine. "I love you too, baby," I responded as I pulled her into my arms. I knew my mother had told me everything about La'Draysha in an effort to lead me back to Shanice, but I had already found everything that I needed with Kim. And unlike Shanice, Kim trusted me completely as her protector. What more could I ask for?

Chapter 30

DANDRIDGE

"Wow, what's this?" Sharon walked into the house where I had left a trail of rose petals from the door all throughout the apartment. I'd purchased some heart shaped paper and wrote on each heart, describing the many reasons why I loved her. "It's what you deserve," I smiled. "I thought you were mad at me," Sharon added as she gave me a grin. "I was but now I want you to forgive me for being a jerk, and for walking around for weeks without speaking to you." She lifted a brow as she picked up each heart and read every message I had written. She smiled slightly at some of them but I could tell she was hesitant, and even a bit leery of my apology. She reached for the very last heart, the one that I held in my hands. "This is the most important one," I said as I handed it to her. She looked into my eyes and read it out loud. "I love you because you brought the truth out of a man everyone thought would be a liar his entire life. Because you are my rock when I need one, and you've shown me how to stop being the man I was, embrace the man I am, and become the man I have the potential to be. I love you because you have taught me what it means to love someone without expectation or condition." She looked up at me. "I love you too, baby daddy," she winked. "Sharon, I want you in my life forever. I want to marry you one day. I don't know when, but I do know that I want that for us and for our son. My mother has done a lot of bad in her life but it seems all of that malice has only lead to good things because without her scheming, I never would have fallen in love with you. But I need you to know that I love you so much that I cannot share you with anyone, man or woman." I was scared to say it because she'd stopped messing with females because they wanted exclusive rights, but I'd never felt for anyone what I felt for Sharon and I needed her to be mine and only mine. "What about more kids? You told me that you never wanted children in the first place, and you already have three. What if I told you I wanted a house full?" Her question caught me off guard. I hadn't realized she wanted more children but I was willing to give her anything she wanted. "We can have a football team if that's what you want." She smiled broadly as she asked another question. "What about going to church? I grew up in church but I stopped going. What if I said I wanted to go back ...as a family?" "Then we'll be there bright and early every Sunday morning," I smiled. I didn't think Sharon was getting the picture. I was ready to be not only the man I needed to be but the man every woman before her had wanted me to be. "Anything else?" I asked with a smile. "No," she said in a whisper as she began to unbutton my shirt. "Just wanted to know you were serious about us." She slowly kissed my neck and I immediately got hard. It had been so long since I'd had sex, I prayed that I wouldn't handle the moment like a teenaged virgin. "Oh, so now you want me?" I joked. "I've wanted you since that night at dinner. I just needed the proof that you wanted me, too," she explained coyly as she unzipped my pants and began massaging my hardness. I closed my eyes, overly satisfied with her touch alone. All of my mom's antics had turned out for my good, even though her intent was to bring harm and pain upon the people around her.

Chapter 31
SHANICE

"**C**an you please answer that!" Reagan yelled at me. "No, I'm not worried about the phone," I snapped. Clearly he could see that I was busy, not to mention purposely ignoring the call. "I'm trying to pack." "Well, whoever it is certainly wants to talk to you," he mused, "and hopefully they can make your ass stay. I don't have anybody but you." He looked sad. "Why don't you call Amy and explain to her that we don't want each other?" His girlfriend had broken up with him after his dumb butt posted a status on Facebook while we were in California. I couldn't understand why he didn't just tell her where he was going in the first place, rather than allowing his location settings to do it for him. Men were so dumb.

"No, I'm good. If she wanted to let the past three years go over a location, then who am I to stop her. It's cool, plenty of females where she came from." Clearly, the man was extremely stubborn I thought, shaking my head. "Okay, well don't complain about being all by yourself then." "This wouldn't even have happened if she would have just moved in with me." I shot him a look. I knew we were only roommates because he was looking for one and his girlfriend was strong in her belief not to shack up but there is no way he didn't think that it would start an issue, him living with another female. I personally didn't care because he and I were just friends, but I had a feeling his girl was going to care and I had been right in my assumptions. My phone rang again and I finally decided to end the calling madness. "Hello?" My voice conveyed annoyance as I answered the call. "Shannie?" The sound of Maxwell's voice left me feeling almost faint. My heart skipped a beat when he said my name, and I could hardly believe my own ears. "Max?" I responded in almost a whisper. He was the last person I had expected to be on the other end of the phone. "Yea, what's up?" He sounded so casual and I played along. "Nothing... just packing." "Packing?" he questioned. "Yeah, I got a place in Boston," I answered, instantly sorry I hadn't interjected more enthusiasm into my response. "Boston? Wow," he replied. "So when do you leave?" "Two days, but the movers will be here in the morning. Is there a reason you called?" As much as I loved hearing his voice, I was already tired of the small talk. "Uh... yeah, two reasons actually. I'm sorry to hear about what La'Draysha tried to do to your grandmother and I hope your mom gets off," he said, pausing a moment before continuing. "I also wanted to see if I could take you to dinner, I guess tonight or tomorrow?" He sounded unsure if he should ask about dinner. "I guess." I tried to sound like it was a bother but I'd still go. "Ok, well which day is good?" "Tomorrow." "Okay. Well, I'll see you tomorrow around seven." "Yep," I responded with little interest again. I didn't want him to think I was sitting around waiting on him to come to his senses. I hung up the phone and started smiling. "That was Maxwell!" I practically yelled at Reagan. "Well, whoop-dee-fucking-do," my roommate responded as he turned back toward the TV where he'd been playing Madden 15. "What's your problem?" "You and your friends in this circle or whatever," he scoffed. "Why don't y'all find some new people to associate yourselves with and move on with your lives? Obviously he doesn't want you, Dan is with your sister ...which is still crazy as hell to me, and you keep judging Tameka's life instead of fixing your own. I hope this relocation to Boston helps you move the fuck on." He had a lot of attitude caught in his throat and I didn't like it. "How do you know he doesn't want me?" Reagan's pessimism was giving me second thoughts about a dinner date with Maxwell. "I'm a man and his actions have proved that to your thirsty ass! You can't even see when a man actually does want you," he accused, throwing the controller down and walking out of the living room toward his bedroom. I didn't know what his issue was, but I didn't like how he'd taken it out on me.

*****

I looked in the mirror, giving myself the once over. I was wearing a black and blue lace dress that stopped more than a few inches above the knees. My breast looked lovely and left very little to the imagination. I had just recently cut my hair into a cute bob and I wore a pair of black stiletto heels. If looks could kill, Maxwell would be dead on sight. My phone rang and I answered it with no hesitation, "Hey." "I'm at your door, been knocking for about three minutes," I heard Maxwell's voice. "Oh I'm sorry. Sometimes it's hard to hear someone knocking from my bedroom. I'm coming now." I hung up the phone, looked at myself one more time, and then headed toward the door. Maxwell was standing there, looking flawless in a pair of khaki pants and a blue and purple stripped button up shirt. His hair was cut in a Mohawk, which made his curls stand out just like the image on his EP album cover. He handed me a single red rose. "You look beautiful," he said, complimenting me. "Thank you. You don't look so bad yourself," I returned the compliment. "Ready?" "As ready as I'm going to be," I smiled, stepping off of the doorstep and walking in the direction of his car. He opened the car door for me as he always did, and we headed to the restaurant. "Big star like you eating at Olive Garden," I smiled at him as we parked. "I still enjoy the simple things in life," he smiled. We walked into the restaurant and that's when I noticed we were the only ones there. "Looks closed," I mused, taking in our surroundings. "It kind of is," he said. "What does that mean?" I was starting to wonder what he was up to, what all of this kindness meant after such an angry exchange of words at the garden gazebo. "Means I talked to a few people and got the restaurant to close tonight so I wouldn't have to be bothered by fans during dinner." "Well, how sweet,"

I blushed. Dan and I had done a lot of things when we were together but never shut down a restaurant. Max and Kim must have had one hell of a breakup, I thought to myself. "So what made you ask me to dinner?" I asked. Immediately, he seemed uncomfortable with my question. "Well, that's kind of hard to answer." "How is it hard?" I was curious to know. "I want us to be friends again, Shanice," he began, "like we were before all of this love stuff got in the way." "Love stuff?" I was insulted. "I didn't mean it offensively. But I don't feel that we should have ever crossed those lines..." Immediately, I interrupted, cutting him off before he could finish. "You've been in love with me since forever, Max! Now you're having a kid and your tune has changed?" "I'm having twins," he said softly, his words feeling like a stab in the gut. Tears came to my eyes but I tried my best to hold them back as I bit my lip and waited for him to continue. "As I was saying, I don't think we ever should have crossed the lines of friendship. You are a beautiful and loving person, but I think you put up with Dan because Harvey was never around to show you what a man should be or how he should treat you. And you didn't know how to be with me because you didn't heal from not only your situation with Dan, but also the trauma of what happened to you. You used me because you knew I loved you." My eyes widened at his accusation and anger flashed in my eyes. "Maxwell, I..." "Shanice, don't say you love me," he warned as he shook his head and continued. "You threw Kim's past up in my face before, but we all have a past. As perfect as you seem to be, you aren't perfect and being in a relationship with you is a lot of work. I pray that you find a man who can stare into those beautiful grey eyes of yours and love you in spite of your flaws, but I am not him. I was someone for you to use just like Dan used you, but I forgive you and as I said earlier, I would like for us to restore our friendship." Tears ran down my cheeks like waterfalls as he spoke and while the truth was hard to bear, I knew that he was right. Max deserved a woman who wanted him because she wanted him rather than because she'd been hurt by other people. "I can't promise you that right now, Max, but maybe in the future," I finally said. "I'll accept that." He smiled and walked around the table to embrace me. What I thought was about to be a dinner to talk about us getting back together had turned into the confirmation that I needed to move forward with my life. Maxwell returned to his seat and for a while, we both ate our food in silence. "Do you think things would have been different if Dan's mom would have left things alone?" I asked. "Probably, but I'm glad they turned out the way they did." He looked down at his empty plate, knowing that those particular words drove the knife in even deeper. "Can we go?" "Yea, I'll take you home." "I think I'll call a cab this time," I decided, pulling out my cell phone just as it started to ring. The screen told me the caller was Tameka. "Hello?" "Girl, you won't believe what happened!" She started talking and I couldn't believe my ears.

Chapter 32

LA'DRAYSHA

I smiled as Nurse Myers entered my room, as she'd been so nice to me these past few months since I'd taken up residence in the hospital. She had replaced the first nurse I was assigned, an incompetent fool who was slow about everything and always interrupted when my mom came to visit. "Do you always have to wear that mask when you come in here, sweetie? Is my cancer contagious?" I asked coyly. "No ma'am. I tell you this every time," the nurse quipped. "I'm a huge germaphobe." "And I ask you this every time... why did you choose to be a Nurse? And how come, when I ask for you after certain hours, people tell me I'm crazy?" I responded. She looked at me but didn't respond. "Have you spoken to your mother lately?" she asked, changing the subject. My cancer had spread to my brain which caused a tumor they told me was inoperable, not to mention I was slowly recovering from a stint of amnesia. They said that I was only seeing my mother due to the tumor. Sometimes the medication would keep her away for a few days, but she always came back when she wanted to see me. "No," I sighed. "I think I made her mad. She wanted me to get rid of Betty Mae." Nurse Myers looked at me as if I'd just confessed to murder. "And what did you tell her?" she asked, raising an eyebrow. "I told her I was done with that family," I stated stubbornly, leaning back on the fresh pillows Nurse Myers had placed behind my back, the coolness seeping through the thin material of my hospital gown. With the arrival of new pillows, my bed was more soft and comfortable. I considered drifting off to sleep ... and that's when mama appeared. "Girl, you shut up. Don't trust this nurse. It's going to end real bad for you," mama warned. I rolled my eyes. I hadn't seen Nurse Myer's face but I trusted her. She made me feel comfortable and seemed to really care as she talked to me about my life and my love for Jamie, who made sure to visit daily. He never stayed real long but I was always glad when he showed up. My brothers had also come by and sent flowers, along with Tina, so I felt like I would truly be missed once I passed away. I hated that I was about to earn my wings, leaving these people who loved me so much. "My mama just told me not to trust you," I told Nurse Myers who also found the warning to be funny. She laughed and the sound was very familiar. It was in that moment, I realized that I'd never really heard her laugh. "Oh, no. You can trust me," she said, assuring me as she walked over to the IV. "The doctor has ordered you a dose of Levaquin." She inserted the needle into the injection port, allowing the medication to circulate through the IV tubing and into my blood stream. My body immediately began to grow numb and within seconds, I could no longer move. "What are you giving me?" I stammered in a voice that was hardly above a whisper. I watched, my body no longer responding, as Nurse Myers pulled another needle from her pocket and removed the cap. I could see it was already filled with some form of liquid. "You won't feel a thing," she promised, lifting the surgical mask she always wore. I looked into her familiar eyes, seeing her for the first time. I couldn't believe she was doing this to me. "Die slowly," she said as she walked away.

Chapter 33

MAXWELL

"I cannot believe that none of her children showed up," my mom said as we stood at La'Draysha's grave side. It had only been me, my mother, Rowland, Bobby, and Jamie in attendance to pay our respects. I looked at my mother but didn't say a word. I knew she was hurt, especially when the autopsy came back revealing the cancer wasn't what had killed her, and the authorities had yet to find the mysterious nurse that drugged her. "Have you spoken to my nephew?" Rowland asked. "No sir. I have remorse toward the situation but I have no reason to speak to Dan." He nodded quietly in understanding. "I wish things would have between different," Bobby said. "Let it go," Jamie said with a hint of attitude. "My sister is dead and you want me to let it go? You probably killed her." "I loved Draysha but you and Rowland didn't even look for her! The two of you were raised by good families and left your sister out in the cold to manage alone and become what she would, so neither one of you can stand here and act like you care," Jamie accused, his face close to Bobby's. "Stop!" my mom yelled. "She is with the Lord now and that's all that matters. "The Lord?" Jamie sneered, eyeing my mom. "You forced God on my wife when she didn't remember that she was no fan of God!" "I didn't force anything on her," my mom replied coolly. "On my last visit to the hospital, she accepted Christ because, although she didn't remember anything ...not even being a mother, she remembered being ready to accept Christ before Melissa got ahold to her." Jamie looked like he could blow a gasket at any time. "You are full of shit," he accused, shaking his head as he walked toward his car. Jamie was a weird dude but I guess that was okay for Miss Harris ...or Mrs. Foster as Jamie would say anytime he heard someone call her by Harris. "May you rest in peace," my mother said as she threw a white lily on top of the casket as it was lowered into the ground. I took her hand in my mine and led her to the car as Bobby and Rowland followed behind us. I couldn't believe the devil had not only passed away but accepted Jesus Christ first. I shook my head and smiled a little at the thought.

Chapter 34

DANDRIDGE

My sisters and I sat at the table in front of the lawyer, waiting on him to begin reading my mother's will. None of us had visited her in the hospital, nor did we attend the funeral because she didn't deserve it. Danae and Carla had both been acting funny ever since the day we received news of a will and I planned to find out why. "We are waiting on Mr. Jamie Foster," her attorney informed us. "Why?" Danae asked as if she didn't know my mother and Jamie were legally married and she had added that man to her will. Mr. Jacobs shot her a look that let her know not to test his patience, as he'd come to do a job and that was it. "Sorry I'm late. I had a funeral to attend," Jamie apologized as he walked in, glaring at the three of us. I shrugged my shoulders. He may have been the sperm donor my mother used but I didn't respect him and he didn't scare me. As soon as Jamie found a chair and was situated, the meeting commenced. "Well, this is going to be very simple," Mr. Jacobs began, as if he expected the meeting to be anything but smooth and simple. "If anyone objects to the decisions made by Miss Harris, excuse me Mrs. Foster," he corrected himself before continuing. "It is a matter that will have to be handled in court. Nothing can be done about any of your grievances today." He passed out envelopes with each of our names on them, written in my mother's handwriting. The letter Mr. Jacobs held in his hands was short and to the point as he read... "To Dandridge Jr., I leave my home, and to each of my children, I leave twenty-five thousand dollars, and to my husband, Jamie, I leave my love." I could have fallen out of my seat with laughter when I realized she had only left Jamie her love. That woman didn't know what love was. Jamie hadn't found the situation nearly as amusing as I had. "That can't be right! I took care of that woman up until the day she died while these ungrateful children did nothing for her. Hell, they didn't even visit her!" "You can have my cut," Danae told him. "I don't want or need anything from the witch." "I'm keeping mine. And uh...

Jamie, you need to start packing, bruh." I laughed even harder. "You might want to find a new freezer for your ice cream. We wouldn't want it to melt," I said as I winked at him, remembering how he'd played me the night we met. He sat back in his seat, speechless and hurt. "Now you see how I felt when I wanted to get to know you," I said as I shook my head and grabbed the letter my mom had written me. I didn't know if I was going to read it or throw it away, only time would tell. "Do you think anyone knows?" I heard Carla whisper to Danae as they started walking toward the exit, Danae already reading her letter. She paused for a moment. "I think she did," her voice sounded a bit fearful. "Who knew what?" I finally asked.

SIX MONTHS LATER
(The Barnes Wedding)

Chapter 35

MAXWELL

I stood beside my mother behind the double doors that would lead her down the aisle and to her waiting groom. She'd invited all of La'Draysha's kids and Shanice's family to the wedding. I encouraged her not to but she felt that with her best friend gone, there should be no reason why everyone couldn't come together peacefully on her big day. "You nervous?" I asked. "How can you tell?" "Because you're about to cut off the circulation in my hand," I laughed. "I'm sorry," she said as she consciously loosened her grip. I opened the door just enough to see who'd shown up and when my eyes landed on Shanice, my heart almost stopped. She looked beyond gorgeous. I thought about the last time I'd seen her. It was the night we'd gotten the news about La'Draysha. She'd actually smiled, although I can't say that I blamed her after all the hell that woman had put her and her family through. Shannie's mom was currently serving an eight year sentence for attempted murder and we were all shocked at how lenient the judge had been with her sentence. I noticed a guy sitting pretty close to her so I assumed it was her man and if it was, I hoped she was happy. Tameka and her man sat next to them and on the other side of Shannie were Dan and Sharon. I still wanted to beat the hell out of Dan but I knew I had to put my feelings to the side for my mother and her special day. Dan's sisters, Danae and Carla, sat directly behind them. "Lord, please let this day go off without a hitch," I prayed under my breath but still loud enough for my mother to hear. "Yes, Lord, please." The doors swung open and the music began, a cue that it was time for me and my mom to take that walk and as nervous as she was, I knew Rowland was good for her and she knew it too. I looked over at the bridesmaids and flashed a smile at Kim, who looked like she could pop at any moment. I'd begged her to sit and watch but she wanted to be a part of my mom's day, just as much as my mom wanted her to be, so she wore flats while the other two bridesmaids wore heels. She smiled back at me and all I could think about was marrying her soon after the babies were born. "Who gives this woman to be married to this man?" the minister asked. "I do," I spoke clearly as I kissed my mother on the cheek and placed her hand in Rowland's. "She's yours now, man," I said. "Take good care of her." "Thank you, son. I will," he promised, flashing me a big smile. I took my seat on the front pew and watched as the songs were sang and the vows exchanged. "You may now kiss your bride," the minister announced as the two of them locked lips and everyone cheered them on. They exited the church and everyone else followed, ready for the reception. "He's got a gun!" I heard someone yell right before shots were fired.

Chapter 36

DANDRIDGE

"No!" I screamed as Sharon's body dropped to the ground. "What fuck is wrong with you?" I screamed, looking up at Jamie with tears in my eyes. I couldn't lose her. I heard people yelling 'Call 911!' but all I could do was hold her. She was carrying another one of my babies and I couldn't lose her or my child. People were running away, exiting the church in all directions, but Maxwell and his family just stood there. "What are you doing?" Rowland asked the gunman calmly. "They know what I'm doing!" He pointed the gun at my sisters, and everyone turned to look at their faces, to make some sense of the situation. "You tell them!" he demanded. "Tell them what you did!" I rocked Sharon back and forth in my arms, praying the ambulance would make it to the church in time. "Your brother is about to lose this bitch if you don't tell them what you did!" He turned and pointed the gun back toward Sharon. I leaned forward, cupping her body, determined to take the next bullet if I had to in order to protect her. "You're drunk and not thinking straight, Jamie. You've just lost your wife and you're heartbroken. Man, put down the gun," Bobby coaxed. "No, I'm thinking more clearly than I ever have. I couldn't figure it out. Draysha was always talking about this nurse and we thought she was crazy ...until my wife turned up dead. Then I remembered her saying to me, 'my mama told me I'm going to die at the hands of one of my children'. I left her for a little while because I felt like she was losing it, and I needed a little time. But shit! Her crazy ass ghost mama was right!" He was now waving the gun in the air and Maxwell was shielding Kim with his life. I wished I'd had the time to shield Sharon. Carla was crying hysterically. "Put down the gun, slowly!" I heard a police officer call out to him. Sharon's eyes had closed but I continued to rock her in my arms and pray. "I will shoot that bitch to make sure she's dead if you don't admit it," he threatened, looking back at Carla and Danae. "Please speak up if you did it," I begged them because I knew it to be true. The letters my mother had written to them both expressed her concern that one of them may hurt her. "Okay, okay, I killed the bitch," Danae admitted with a stone cold look on her face. Jamie turned toward her and pulled the trigger, her body dropped to the ground as Maxwell tackled Jamie from his blind side and the police moved in. Jamie was in cuffs and the paramedics were pulling Sharon from my arms. No one rushed to Danae's side. It was clear that she was gone. I looked at Carla but couldn't say a word as I followed the paramedics to the ambulance where they quickly loaded Sharon and I climbed in behind her. Jamie must have really loved my mother, I thought, as tears rolled down my cheeks. I watched Jamie being placed in handcuffs and shoved into the back of a squad car as the ambulance doors closed us in.

Chapter 37

SHANICE

"Is she alright?" I looked up to see Maxwell walking into Sharon's room. Dan looked like he was too hurt and distraught to acknowledge the bad blood that had previously kept him and Max apart. Another scene was the last thing Sharon needed. Dan must have been thinking the same thing. "She's going to recover but the baby didn't make it," I answered, lowering my voice for fear that Sharon might overhear. She wouldn't be told about the baby until she regained consciousness. Dan also needed to be the one that told her. "I'm so sorry, man." Max looked at Dan and placed a vase full of roses on the stand next to her bed. The air was awkward between them but Max placed one hand on Dan's shoulder for a moment before pulling it away. "I'm just happy she's alive, but I'm not ready to tell her we lost our baby," Dan responded to him and the room fell silent for a while. I held onto Sharon's hand as she slept and the three of us looked at one another. Reagan was waiting on me at the hotel because I didn't really want him around my family in a time like this. He meant well but he could be a real drama queen at times. My grandmother had visited and anointed the room and its threshold with oil, and prayed with us that the pain and suffering that Miss Harris left behind would come to an end. I couldn't believe that, even in death, La'Draysha was still hurting people ...or at least someone who loved her was hurting people. "My mom said she'll handle things for you with Danae," Maxwell said in an almost whisper, unsure if he should mention Danae's funeral arrangements or wait until later. "Tell her I said thank you," Dan mumbled, staring into space. "She didn't do it, you know," he added as he began to cry again, covering his eyes with his hand. "She said she did it," I said, confused. "Carla did it. The girls told me," he shook his head in disbelief. "I can't believe she did that. Danae confessed to save Carla. I shouldn't have told them to tell Jamie what they..." His voice trailed off. My eyes widened. Carla was the sweetest and most pleasant of the three sisters. I couldn't believe that she'd do something like that. Maxwell placed his hand on Dan's shoulder again. "We've had our differences but anything you need, man." Dan looked up at him. "I know." "Life is too short. I just want both of you to know that I love y'all," Max spoke from the heart as he looked at us and in that moment, it felt as if none of the drama in our past was important anymore. Dan stood and embraced Max and they held each other for what seemed like forever. I looked away as tears welled up in my eyes and I reflected on how overwhelmingly emotional the day had been. I was surprised at how good it felt to see Max and Dan repair their friendship and in the moment, I could easily forget the pain both of them had caused me. They both stretched one free arm in my direction, inviting me to join. "Shannie, if you don't get over here and get in on this...," Dan began. I didn't give him time to finish his sentence as I quickly obliged him by joining the group hug. It felt like the three of us were back together again, except this time as three old friends.

THE END

SNEAK PEEK

Teri Woods
presents
Having Your Brothers Back Can be The
My Brother's Keeper
Reason He Lives to See Another Day
Book IIII A Novel
w York Times Be
Billie Dureyca Shell

MY BROTHER'S KEEPER

BOOK IIII

A Novel

Billie Dureyea Shell

Chapter 1

THE GENERAL

The General looked around his office, pondering his next move on the rebels. The rebel army had caused more problems within his smuggling business as of late. While he was out of the country trying to secure the African Black Diamond as his brother, also the South African president, had commanded. The rebels had raided his military artillery camps, taking whatever they could grab. He didn't receive any of the money promised from his brother because he'd failed to bring home the diamond. His next move had to be great, or the president would have his head put on a stake. The General watched people move about through his massive office window. He heard a knock at the door. He didn't bother walking over to ask who was interrupting his time of peace. "It's open, lieutenant." He continued to face the outside world. His mind moved to another place after the death of his father. The diamond was the cause of his murder, and the General would do anything to retrieve the precious stone, even if it meant going against his brother's rule. "General," the lieutenant stepped into the office. "My apologies for interrupting. I've come to ask how you wish to proceed with the rebels?" It was a question that he couldn't avoid with everything that had happened up until this point. Mainly with his brother putting an end to their field supplies. The army needed more weapons to deal with the rebels. He didn't have enough guns to supply all of his men. If he decided to move forward and attack the rebels, some would attend the battle without a weapon to fire. Instead, they would have to make use of knives, grenades, spears, or whatever they could construct to defend themselves. His army outnumbered the rebels, but the outcome would be intensely felt due to the number of casualties they would suffer in a war with another country. If only he had a replacement for Bill Right, the man he knew as Jar Simmons. "How would you like us to deal with the situation, Abrafo?" The General asked his most trusted comrade. For years, they had known each other since they were kids, training to become soldiers in the African military. The General excelled in war strategy while Abrafo exceeded in kills. And that's what his name stands for . . . executioner. The General gave Abrafo his name after learning about his family history. They were assassins, and the name Abrafo suited him well. It was the General's way of protecting his only friend's identity. "You are our leader," Lieutenant Abrafo replied. "It would be wise for you to give the command, not me. I am a man of war, and you are a man of approach. Your tactic will be far more effective than mine." The General turned from the window to face Abrafo. "Do you think it would be wise to start a war with the rebels?" The General wanted to test the lieutenant to see his view of their unfortunate circumstance. It didn't take long for Abrafo to understand what the General asked of him. The General wouldn't ask a third time for his opinion. "No, General." The answer was short, the way he intended for it to be, knowing a why question would follow. "Why do you feel as such?" The General asked curiously. Abrafo didn't become a high-ranking lieutenant by being a cretinous man. The army had to confront the rebels from a different standpoint, and the General needed a fresh perspective. Abrafo was more than a killer to him. He would be the General's new plan of action until his mind was off the diamond. He couldn't lead his men into a war without a clear sense of reason. "The rebels are growing strong in numbers," the lieutenant said evenly. "And they're confident now that they have successfully raided our camps for weapons. We will lose more soldiers than intended if we face them without first breaking their spirit." "Break their spirit," the General folded his hands behind his back. "And how would you suggest proceeding without a battle?" The lieutenant took a short moment to think about an answer. If he replied quickly, the General would possibly void his response. He looked to be deep in thought. His explanation had to be clear of mistakes and thoughtful. He spoke when formulating the right choice of words. "The same way you stop a fire-breathing dragon." The General smiled at Abrafo. "We cut off the head." Abrafo balled his first and placed it over his heart. "For Africa." The General followed suit. "For Africa."

Chapter 2

KANE

"How much longer," Smoke sounded from the seat across from mine. "It's been hours, and my legs feel paralyzed." I looked back at my friend and smiled. Honestly, I was happy he could move his legs at all. Adrian had shot him in the leg, and Smoke had to use a cane to stand up straight for a week. At first, I thought he would never be the same, but that was just me worrying too much. My guy pulled through just fine. "It's not that bad," Kim said. "We'll get there in the next thirty minutes or so. Sit back and relax, crybaby." Smoke threw his head back on the seat rest, frustrated. I shook my head and turned my attention back to the map I had picked up in a store at the airport. We were on our way to Africa. Even Big Bruce decided to come with us. I told him it could get ugly, and he was still down to ride. None of us were in trouble with the law, so I booked a commercial flight straight to Tripoli, Libya. It cost me $1500 a ticket. Not that it mattered, but damn, I know now why people save money for vacations. This was my first time leaving the country, and it felt good to get away even though I was traveling to find my mother. I didn't have my father's black notebook anymore. It would've been helpful because it had names and locations. The only thing I had to lean on was the map in my father's office. There were pinned locations that corresponded with the notebook. That's how I figured out my mother would be somewhere in Libya. It's where my father built his organization and headquarters. Where I assume he stored the money and weapons. The only thing I couldn't figure out was why my mother chose Jordan over me? We could've done this together. "How long are you gonna stare at that map?" Kim asked. "What are you trying to figure out that we don't know already?" "Roads, places," I gave her a short answer. "Studying the landscape." "Why," she asked and leaned her head against my shoulder. "One, I think it'd be best if I at least know where we're at," I informed her. "And two, I'm searching for an unoccupied area away from the city. Somewhere, a plane can land without being noticed by the army." "I thought your father worked with the army?" I looked around and saw several people staring at us. Mostly Africans, heading back to their homeland after visiting America. After Kim said, your father worked with the army; we caught ugly glares from everyone who heard. "Keep your voice down," I whispered. "I don't think foreigners should be talking about the army." She secretly looked around and spotted the people with hard eyes on us. "Right." "Anyway," I began. "I wasn't talking about Libya's army. I was talking about rebel armies who'd love to get their hands on money and weapons. My father would've avoided those areas to prevent any problems." "What if he paid them off," she remembered to speak with a low voice. "It's possible," I said. "But why spend extra money when you can just stay off the grid?" My father wouldn't work with them knowing they were against the army—too much of a headache." "For you," she replied. "I think like him," I smiled. "Whatever, smart guy," she kissed my cheek. I believe it to be true that my father wouldn't work with a malicious group. The notebook had names of Generals and prominent figures written in it. He was larger than life, and it would take more than a few soldiers to protect what he built. He used to tell me, don't work hard at something if you're gonna half-ass in the end? I wouldn't do it, so why would he? The only thing I ever smuggled was contraband from one cell to another when I was locked up. The guards didn't allow inmates to trade anything, so we had to move low-key. I met a guy who would watch my cell while I was on free time for a pack of cigarettes a week. Inmates would sneak into your cell and steal goods while you were away watching TV or occupied in the yard. After it happened to me once, I knew that I had to hire help. I paid a killer to watch over other inmates with sticky fingers, and it worked. This situation was no different. My father hired the army so he could move freely on the land, but that didn't mean the rebels wouldn't try their hand. If you build a restaurant around rats, they'll eat your food. That's how I look at it. And . . . there are plenty of rats where we're going, if you know what I mean.

Chapter 3
ABEL

bel checked his watch and smiled. Silva had successfully landed the plane in Africa. They had touchdown just past the border of Mali. Abel looked around the area through the side window and saw the desert go on for miles. The sand and dirt covering the area appeared to be endless, and he had already begun to feel the heat beaming down from the sun. He stood when the plane came to a complete stop, opting to sit in the back to keep a close eye on Silva and Britt. "How hot is it?" Gina stood and wiped the sweat from her forehead. The heat made her want to ask Silva to fly them back home. She had never experienced a high temperature at this level, and it was more than enough to get her frustrated. "It's one hundred and five degrees," Snake answered exasperatedly.

"What the fuck," Gina muttered at nobody in particular. "I'm getting woozy," Bam stood and dropped back into the seat. "I don't know if I can do this. It's too hot for me to think straight." Gina formed a disgusted expression on her face when she looked at Bam. It was her moment to comment on his weakness, but receiving a response would've gotten her even angrier in combination with the sun. The heat provided her enough irritation to deal with for now. "Get yourself together," Abel told Bam before opening the plane's side door. He immediately felt a strong breeze of heat attack his entire body as if an unknown entity forced it. The fury of wind lasted a short span before he was able to step off the aircraft. Abel held up his hand and spotted a large dome tent and a 4x4 off-road jeep. The campsite appeared invisible from the air. It was the perfect color for someone who wished to camouflage it with the surrounding landscape. Silva turned off the engine and followed the others off the plane. He stood next to Abel and pointed at the dome tent. "Dat a ih." Mali was the closest destination Silva could land without the army noticing the aircraft. Abel knew this to be true with the amount of illegal activity that had taken place throughout the years. If he desired a safe and secure landing, Mali was the only option without the plane getting shot down. He turned to Bam and Snake. "Unload the supplies." Bam spoke up, "What about her?" his eyes were on Gina, wondering why Abel didn't ask her to help. "Shut up, you idiot," Snake eyed Bam. Abel didn't bother to turn around when he spoke. "I want you to be alive when I return." Bam was mind-boggled with Abel's response. His words rang out in his mind . . . I want you to be alive when I return. Bam planned to murder Gina before leaving America, and he knew that she carried the same intentions. Abel was right. They couldn't be left alone together, not even for a second. He sucked his teeth and followed Snake back inside the plane. Gina smirked at Bam as he turned away, thinking his time would come. Keep on, tough guy, she thought. Hiding her anger toward Bam was becoming a daily task. When Abel no longer needs Bam, he's dead. He was at the top of her to-kill list, without a doubt. Britt stepped beside Abel. "I noticed you're in pain while on the plane. Is everything alright with you?" She had a concerned look on her face. Gina bumped Britt out of her way and stood next to Abel. "He's fine," she snarled. "Let's go inside. It's fucking hot out here." She held Abel's arm and guided him toward the tent. Silva witnessed the tension between Gina and Britt. He was still unaware of how Britt felt about Abel. She hadn't shown any signs of feelings for him until now. "Blurtnawt," he muttered, walking past Britt. Abel stopped at the tent's door, waiting for Silva to catch up and lead the way inside. "After you," he smiled at Silva as if opening the door would spring a trap. "Yah mon," Silva pulled back the opening, showing there was nothing to fear. After stepping inside, he called to the man sitting Indian-style on a throw rug in front of them. "Oyoo." Oyoo opened his eyes and stared at them. He had a mean expression on his face as though they disrupted his concentration while meditating. After a short moment of studying the other unknown guests, he smiled at his friend. "Silva," Oyoo sounded excited and stood to greet him. Abel stood firm by the door with Gina as the two men shook hands. He kept his eyes on Oyoo the entire time while on high alert. If he missed any potential threats, Gina would take care of it. That's why he wanted her to come inside with him. Her awareness was greater than Bam and Snake's put together, which kept him at ease. Oyoo looked over Silva's shoulder and spoke. "That man reminds me of someone. Who is he?" Silva turned around and faced Abel. "Di dead mon son." Oyoo's eyes widened. "Jar," he said in shock. He stepped closer to Abel. "Have you come to take his place?" Oyoo noticed Abel's muscular physique, and the man was by far larger than his father. Oyoo worked with Jar for more than twenty years as a driver. When beginning the smuggling business, Silva and Oyoo were Jar's first transportation hires. Jar cared for them to the point that there wasn't a need to work for anyone else. Even after Jar's death, the men were well off, but they loved making money and stayed in business as contractors for anyone looking to transport. Abel scanned Oyoo as he approached, noticing he was a man of the land who could speak perfect English. He was surprised by that and how well kept it was inside the tent. He expected it to be dusty and hot. It was neither, and somehow the sun rays didn't affect the inside temperature. "I haven't decided as of yet." "Then why have you come, son of Jar?" Oyoo looked at Abel's chest and felt his pain. It was a gift he possessed that allowed him to sense the aura surrounding the body. "I've come for the General," Abel answered truthfully. "I have a gift for him." Oyoo smiled sarcastically. "A gift for the General. The man who brings war to his people." Oyoo turned away from Abel. "What gift do you bring, if not weapons? He values his army, and your father made a business of it. Your gift will get you killed." "I beg to differ," Abel said confidently. "I have something he's been searching for." Oyoo turned around and thought, could he possibly have it? There was only one thing the General would accept besides weapons. And that would be the African Black Diamond. He was well aware of the rebels raiding the campsites. The General announced that anyone who worked with the rebels would be killed. "You have it?" Abel signed with a slight nod. "Okay, I will lead you to the General, but I will not reveal myself," Oyoo said, hiding his true intentions. He pointed to Abel's chest. "I will show you to a doctor before we go. You will need all of your strength, son of Jar."

Chapter 4

JORDAN

Noti looked at the surrounding area and noticed a plane at their landing spot. It's been several years since she returned to the landing zone. It was one of many locations Jar used for travel. She remembered meeting Oyoo with her husband at a bar in Bamako. Oyoo worked as a tour guide and offered to show them around the city. Jar accepted, and the next day Oyoo picked them up from a hotel. They toured the entire town, and Jar was impressed with Oyoo's sense of direction and driving skills. It was enough for Jar to extend a proposal for Oyoo to be part of the business. Noti thought about landing the plane anyway but quickly decided it wouldn't be a good idea. Her husband was dead, and she figured Oyoo had found a new boss. Nobody knew who she was except

Oyoo, and whoever it was visiting might not be friendly. They were in dangerous waters, and steering clear of violence was the key to staying alive a day longer. "We need to land at another location." "I thought this was the location," Adrian spoke up from the pilot's seat. "I don't see anywhere else to land." Rick sat in the back of the plane next to Jordan. He'd never been more terrified in his life. Jordan and his brother Adrian were monsters. After Jordan woke up, he became himself again, and the FBI agent was gone. He lashed out at Adrian for knocking him over the head. Adrian could've wrecked the plane if Noti and Rick didn't stop him in time. Jordan kept his eyes on his brother for most of the trip. Rick thought if he closed his eyes for a second, they all be dead. Sleep was not an option either, and he damn near didn't blink. "Land this fucking plane," Jordan growled at Adrian. "You said this was the spot, and now you've changed your mind all of a sudden. That's not gonna work for me. This flight is over." He stared at Noti hard. She somehow became the bandleader, which didn't sit right with him. She'd be useless if he could get her to give up the safe location and the passcode. Striking that kind of luck would end her life, and he knew it wouldn't happen. He'd never get the information, not if she desired to live. Jordan's frustration dictated his actions, and until he regained control of the situation, his goal was to piss them off. "Never mind the plane," Noti said evenly. "And prepare yourself for a fight. That's the only option if we land now." "She's right," Rick spoke up. He noticed the aircraft and spotted two men unloading luggage. "Well, we have to land soon," Adrian checked the gasoline level meter. "We're running short on fuel." They had to miss a fuel station because a police boat docked nearby. He couldn't risk it and let the last opportunity pass by. Jordan began to spaz out, letting his emotion run wild. "Fuck!" he roared and started to destroy anything in reach. "How are we runnin' short on fuel?" He tossed random items to the front of the plane. He picked up a glass of water and threw it at the front window, just missing Adrian. "Goddammit!" "Someone calm his ass down," Adrian shouted and took a split second to glance back at Jordan. That would've been the last straw if the glass hit him. Jordan was pushing it to the maximum limit, and Adrian was more than ready to do something harmful to his brother, even if it meant ending his arrangement with Noti. Rick turned his attention from the plane below and focused on his former partner. "Shit," he muttered and tried to defuse Jordan's outrage. He held up his hands and blocked Jordan from throwing more items toward the cockpit. "Are you trying to kill us?" "Get the hell out of my way, Rick." Jordan had the devil inside of him and wasn't afraid to show it. The Planner was the cause of his outrage. It wasn't his fault the plane was running out of fuel. It wasn't his fault Noti was the one in control. It wasn't his fault Rick had to tag along with them. So many different things began to fester inside his head, and he wanted to break loose. Freeing himself from everyone and unleashing his anger was the only way to do it. It made him feel good, and Rick kept trying to stop that sensation. "I can't let you distract your brother from landing this plane safely." Rick kept his hands up and continued to block Jordan's path. Why did I get myself into this, he thought. He wouldn›t be in this predicament if he only called for backup when discovering the cabin. Obey the rules as an officer and follow protocol. That's all it takes, and he failed to do both when Adrian apprehended him in the woods. Jordan suddenly felt exhausted, and he just stood there, staring at Rick like a madman. His chest heaved in and out, taking in deep breaths of air. He needed water before he passed out from dehydration. It was hot, and his energy output didn't agree with the heat from the sun. He looked at the cooler on the side of the seat. Hopefully, there was another bottle of water inside. He reached for it, and Rick reacted by moving in his way. "Get the hell out of my way. I need a drink." Rick sighed and looked at the cooler. "Okay," he moved to the side. Jordan opened the cooler and cracked open a water bottle. He tossed the cap at Rick's chest, and it bounced off to the ground. He smirked at him, "Rookie." The whole time Jordan was having a fit, Noti focused on the plane below. The men appeared to be Americans. Maybe they were smugglers who prospered after her husband's death. When a king is dead, a new one will rise in any case. The luggage couldn't carry the number of weapons it takes to feed one rebel group. There could be a second plane, or money was in the bags. Suddenly, a woman and Oyoo emerged from the tent. Her eyes were sharp enough to assure it was him. She learned to see from a flying distance in the beginning stages of Jar's operation. He wasn't the only one taking risks for their future. It can't be, she thought. Another figure emerged from the dome tent. Noti was stunned after realizing a demon had followed her to Africa. As the plane passed over the location, she could've sworn Abel looked into the aircraft and made eye contact with her. She fell back from the window in shock. Her heart rate began to speed up a notch, and she felt like it would explode. Abel could have caused her to have a mild heart attack. She put her hand over her chest in fear. Rick caught her from falling to the ground before speaking to her worriedly. "Are you okay?" "No," she answered seriously. "The devil has arrived."

ABOUT THE AUTHOR

New York Times & International Best Selling Author
Billie Dureyea Shell was born in Compton California and now
lives in Ladera Heights with his wife and
kids who he loves to spend time with.
He is the Owner of several properties in the Los Angeles area
and gives back to his community by providing low income
housing to those who need it.
He stated "It doesn't matter where you at or where you from
it's what you do with your time. There's nothing you can't do
if you put your mind to it".